Into the Arms of His Boss

Lock Down Publications and Ca$h
Presents
Into the Arms of His Boss
A Novel by *Jamila*

Into the Arms of His Boss

Lock Down Publications
P.O. Box 944
Stockbridge, Ga 30281

Visit us at
www.lockdownpublications.com

Copyright 2020 by Jamila
Into the Arms of His Boss

First Edition November 2020
Printed in the United States of America

This is a work of fiction. Names, characters, places, and incidents either are products of the author's imagination or are used fictitiously. Any similarity to actual events or locales or persons, living or dead, is entirely coincidental.

Lock Down Publications
Like our page on Facebook: Lock Down Publications @
lications @
www.facebook.com/lockdownpublications.ldp
Cover design and layout by: **Dynasty Cover Me**
Book interior design by: **Shawn Walker**
Edited by: **Shamika Smith**

Jamila

Stay Connected with Us!

Text **LOCKDOWN** to 22828 to stay up-to-date with new releases, sneak peaks, contests and more…

Thank you!

Submission Guideline.

Submit the first three chapters of your completed manuscript to ldpsubmissions@gmail.com, subject line: Your book's title. The manuscript must be in a .doc file and sent as an attachment. Document should be in Times New Roman, double spaced and in size 12 font. Also, provide your synopsis and full contact information. If sending multiple submissions, they must each be in a separate email.

Have a story but no way to send it electronically? You can still submit to LDP/Ca$h Presents. Send in the first three chapters, written or typed, of your completed manuscript to:

LDP: Submissions Dept
P.O. Box 944
Stockbridge, Ga 30281

DO NOT send original manuscript. Must be a duplicate.

Provide your synopsis and a cover letter containing your full contact information.

Thanks for considering LDP and Ca$h Presents.

Jamila

Acknowledgment

First, I'd like to thank God for helping me discover my talent in writing and guiding me through this difficult but rewarding journey. I'd like to thank my family and friends for their never-ending love and support. I want to give a shout out to my fellow alumni and the current students of Dougherty Comprehensive High School of Albany, Georgia, and Savannah State University of Savannah, Georgia. I also want to thank my readers, who have been with me since day one during my Cynthia Blue days. You guys are my everything! I appreciate you giving my books a chance, giving me feedback, and encouraging me to keep pushing. Thank you, Ca$h and Coffee for believing in me and giving me straight with no chaser type of advice. Thank you to the rest of the LDP family for the love and support. I also wanna give a special shout out to S. Allen for keeping me on my toes, encouraging me to never give up and to always keep pushing. I hope y'all like this romantic drama. I hope it entertains and educates because I'm gonna let y'all know right now this series is gonna have y'all all up in y'all feelings. Also, it takes place in my hometown of Albany, Georgia. Actually, this is the first book I've ever written that takes place in my hometown of Albany, Georgia. This book is near and dear to my heart. I hope y'all like what I came up with and will continue to ride with me while supporting me in the future. Enjoy! *hugs and kisses*

P.S. My inbox is always open if y'all want to discuss the book, let me know how you feel and/or cuss me out LOL!

Dedication

I'd like to dedicate this project to anybody who has been affected by domestic violence in any way, shape, or form. If you or a loved one is currently suffering from domestic violence, get help ASAP! Don't let shame silence you! Like the saying goes: Closed mouths don't get fed. Well, silent screams don't get saved. So please if you need help, scream before the day comes that you can't!

Jamila

Into the Arms of His Boss

Prologue

"Dana! What the fuck do you think you are doing?" Neil asked with anger in his voice while witnessing his fiancée and the mother of his unborn child zipping up her last bag in the master bedroom they no longer shared together.

"What the fuck does it look like I'm doing?" Dana barked out her answer and grabbed her bag. "I'm packing my shit and leaving your ass! Something I should've done a long time ago!" She brushed past Neil, walked out the door and down the stairs.

"Stop being so fucking overly dramatic so we can talk about this!" Neil ordered as he followed Dana down the stairs.

"We ain't got shit to talk about!" Dana's mind was completely made up. She was officially done with this nigga's abuse, lies, deceits, deceptions, disrespect, and community dick. There was no changing her mind. She had reached her breaking point with this abusive fuck boy that she had no business giving a second of her time to. "That shit you pulled was unforgivable!"

Neil grabbed Dana's arm firmly. "And I told your ass I was sorry!"

Dana snatched her arm away from Neil's tight grip. "You're only sorry that your no-good ass got caught! This is it! I'm done! It's over! I'm leaving your motherfucking ass and I'm taking my baby with me!" she referred to the seven-month-old fetus growing inside of her.

Whap!

Neil gave Dana a hard back-handed slap making her fall on the floor and drop her bag. "You ain't going nowhere! You understand that shit, bitch?"

Neil pounced on top of Dana and started beating her like she was a man. He punched her repeatedly in the face and all over her body.

"Stop! Please stop!" Dana tried to block the blows with her arms but to no avail. Neil's rage was on autopilot.

Neil grabbed Dana by her hair and screamed in her face. "Shut the fuck up! You ungrateful bitch!" And delivered another punch to her right eye.

"Stop! I'm carrying our baby!" Neil ignored Dana's desperate pleas for her and her unborn baby's life by continuing to beat her like she was less than nothing.

Dana leaned over on her left side in pain and Neil began to kick her in the chest and back. "You wanna leave me!"

Kick!

"Huh!" After a few more kicks, Neil stopped kicking Dana. He caught his breath and came up with a devilish idea. "If you wanna leave that motherfucking bad, go ahead and leave then bitch! I'll even drop your worthless hoe ass off!" He yanked Dana off the floor. "Now take off your clothes!"

What the fuck? Dana had no idea Neil was this crazy, but then again maybe she should've known by the obvious red flags throughout their entire relationship. "Neil, please don't..."

Neil cut her off with another pimp slap to the face. "Bitch take off your motherfucking clothes now!" Neil let Dana go and she managed to maintain her balance. She was quivering with fear as she began to undress. "Hurry your dumb ass up!" Dana picked up the pace until her naked bruised body was completely exposed.

"Let's go!" Neil yanked Dana's arm and dragged her towards the front door.

"Where are we going?" Dana stuttered with fright.

Neil answered Dana's question by slamming her head on the coffee table knocking her out. He dragged Dana outside and threw her body in the trunk of his car. He got in his driver's seat and went on to his destination. It took about thirty minutes for Neil to find the perfect spot. He found a path that led to the woods and followed it. When he felt like he was deep enough in the forest, Neil stopped the car.

Neil got out and popped the trunk. Dana was still unconscious. He picked up Dana's body and threw her towards the trees like he was disposing of some trash.

"Good riddance, bitch!" Neil chuckled and got back in his car and drove off like nothing happened as the rain started to pour down.

Jamila

Chapter 1
Seven Months Earlier

How in the fuck did I end up here? Twenty-three-year-old Dana K'Mya Spicer sighed as she looked in the mirror getting ready to go to some party Neil told her about. She didn't have to apply a lot of makeup now because the bruises were finally healed from Neil's last flare-up.

Dana did not picture this being her life after graduating from Albany State University cum laude and landing a good job at the United States Post Office. That all changed when she got in deep with Neil. She was forced to quit her job and the relationship was like walking on eggshells. Now, they're engaged and recently found out they're gonna be parents. Since the news of the pregnancy, the beatings have stopped. Dana just hoped it'll stay that way after the baby is born and things will change.

After perfecting her makeup and hair, Dana stood in the full body mirror admiring her looks. She stood 5'5", one hundred and forty-eight pounds, long black hair, light brown skin complexion, and hazel brown eyes. The powder blue stretch pantsuit looked good on her.

As she was making herself some iced tea, Neil walked through the door. He sat his work gear on the living room floor. Neil Carlos Henderson at age twenty-six, was a successful businessman. He stood at 6'3", two hundred and forty pounds solid, dark brown skin complexion, clean shaved and baldheaded. He was a manager at Georgia Power. He also made smart and sound investments when it came to the NYSE (New York Stock Exchange). His success is the reason they lived in a Victorian Style, two-story house on the wealthy side of Albany, Georgia. He looked at his fiancée and smiled.

"Baby, you're looking great tonight," Neil commented while walking through the kitchen. He kissed her on the right cheek.

Dana winced, not sure what he was about to do. Her reaction caught him somewhat off guard.

"Dana, are you okay?" he asked.

She smiled uneasily. "I'm okay." She grabbed another glass, put some ice in it, and poured him some tea. "So, what's up with this party we're going to?"

Neil grabbed the glass of iced tea out of her hand. He took a sip and sighed as the soothing liquid traveled down his throat. "My boss, Mr. Nicholas Washington, invited us to a dinner party at his house." He finished the tea and set the glass on the kitchen counter. "I've got to go get ready. The party starts at nine."

Neil walked out of the kitchen, heading to the shower.

Dana put the two glasses in the dishwashing machine and placed the tea back in the refrigerator. While waiting for the dishwasher to finish washing and rinsing, she thought about the last fight she and her fiancé had. It was right before she found out she was pregnant. Neil had beaten her so badly that she ended up having to go to the emergency room.

The fight had started over the way some random guy had looked at and spoken to her during their night out at Ruby Tuesday's. She, being friendly, had smiled and spoken back to the fairly decent looking young man. It was completely innocent, but it didn't matter to Neil. Once they'd gotten home, Neil's mood changed. And without saying a word, he had jumped on her. He'd beaten her with his fist like she was some nigga on the street he had beef with.

Dana had suffered a fractured right jaw, a broken nose, and a black eye. The pain she'd felt wasn't so much from the actual physical abuse being done to her body. Her pain derived from the illusion of love. Dana was scared, not naïve.

Her train of thought was broken by Neil's presence. He'd gotten dressed for the occasion, and was looking good in his smoke gray slacks, black short sleeve turtleneck shirt, and low-cut casual Timberlands to Dana. So good that she had to compliment him.

"Mr. Henderson, you know how to put on when you want to," she said.

Neil wasn't smiling. He stared at Dana coldly while putting on his Citizen timepiece and other jewelry. "Try not to embarrass me tonight. Do you understand what I'm saying, Dana?"

She quickly nodded her head. "Yes, I understand Neil."

A smirk was plastered on his face. "If you know what's best for you and the baby, you'll continue to understand. Now, let's go."

Jamila

Chapter 2

"Are you okay, baby?" Neil asked Dana with concern when they arrived at their destination.

"Yes," Dana answered trying to brush off what Neil said to her before they left.

They got out of Neil's black Jaguar and entered the house arm and arm looking like a power couple. The house was huge and well decorated filled with people mingling and enjoying themselves.

"This is a nice house," Dana complimented.

"Yes, it is," Neil agreed.

"There's Mr. Washington." Neil pointed at a handsome, six foot three, two hundred and sixty pounds of muscular, dark brown, thirty-three-year-old man approaching them.

"Neil, glad you could make it," Mr. Washington greeted.

"Yes sir," Neil said with gratitude. He glanced over at Dana and went on to make the introduction. "Mr. Washington, I'd like you to meet..."

"Dana!" Mr. Washington exclaimed with excitement.

"Endz, is that you?" Dana had a big smile on her face and blurted out Mr. Washington's nickname.

"Yes, it's me." Endz flashed his perfect smile and pulled Dana into a hug. "It's great to see you."

Neil was struggling to fight off his inner jealousy towards witnessing Endz and Dana's embrace. Since Endz is part owner of his place of employment he had to keep his cool. "You two know each other?"

"Since we were kids," Dana answered. "Endz and my big brother, Eli, were best friends back in the day."

Endz and Eli were thick as thieves growing up. They also hustled together on the low. Endz was both book smart and street smart. He graduated with honors at Dougherty Comprehensive High School and Morehouse College. Together, he and Eli made one hell of a team. Endz was the brains and Eli was the muscle. Eventually, they were able to go legit and everything was all good until Eli ended up murdered outside the club two months after his thirtieth birthday.

"Let's sit down," Endz offered Neil and Dana a seat on the vacant couch. His first question was for Dana. "How you been? The last I heard you were working at the post office."

"Yes, I was." Dana nodded.

"You still there?"

"No."

"What happened with that?"

"Long story." Dana really didn't wanna get into the details of why she had to leave the job she loved so much. It was a long and humiliating story that she would rather forget.

"Gotcha." Endz went on to the next question. "How long have y'all been together?"

"About two years," Neil answered. "We're engaged." He lifted up Dana's left hand to show Endz the blinging eighteen carats, white gold, diamond ring on her ring finger.

"Congratulations," Endz said.

"And expecting." Neil rubbed Dana's stomach.

"Say what?" Endz was blown away. "My black ass is way out of the loop. I wonder why Ant didn't mention it." Antoinette Morris-Spicer, better known as Ant, is Eli's widow and the mother of his two children. Connie and Eli Junior. She owns a few beauty supply stores and is now thinking about selling hair care products and wigs. "When was the last time you talked to her?"

"About two weeks ago," Dana answered. "She and the kids are doing great."

"She said she's about to open another store soon."

"I keep telling her to take her business online," Dana said. "I even made a few suggestions on some shipping methods she could use."

"Neil." Endz got his attention. "You got a brilliant, special, and lovely lady right here." He pointed at Dana.

"With a woman like this on your arm, you can go anywhere you want in life. All the way to the motherfucking top!"

"You are absolutely right." Neil pulled Dana into his arms and held her tight. "I love this woman and she is all mine." He planted a kiss on her.

"Dana, you need to be on my team," Endz said.

"Me?" Dana wasn't expecting anything like this.

"Yes, and I have the perfect job for you. I need a Shipping Operations Manager to help my companies out with their orders, shipments, and their delivery systems. That's right up your alley. It'll just be like working at the post office. Except you'll be paid more money and you'll have a boss you're cool with." Endz was making the job offer hard to turn down and that was his plan.

"This is an amazing offer." Dana would love to work again. She didn't want to depend on Neil forever. Especially if his abuse doesn't stop. At least until she's twenty-five when she'll be able to have access to her inheritance from Eli. A detail she 'neglected' to tell Neil about. "Are you sure?"

"Yes, Dana. Take the offer. For me?" Endz smoothly begged.

Dana turned to Neil and asked. "What do you think?" She didn't wanna risk making him angry. She knew he wasn't stupid enough to try anything in a house full of witnesses, but she also didn't wanna be subjected to another ass whooping when they got home.

"Baby, say yes. You can do it," Neil encouraged.

"Alright, I will," Dana accepted.

"Welcome to the team," Endz said.

"Congratulations baby." Neil hugged and kissed Dana.

"Dana! Dana Spicer, is that you?"

Dana turned around to see who called her name. It was a twenty-five-year-old, five foot five, one hundred and fifty-five-pound, beautiful espresso skin toned woman with her jet black hair in goddess cornrows. "Dominique Scott! What's up girl?" she cheered with excitement at the sight of her best friend and her first roommate from their days at Albany State University. "How you been?" The ladies hugged.

"I've been good," Dominique pulled Dana to the side so they

can talk. "How about you?"

"I'm good. I just got hired by Endz, literally a few minutes ago." Dana was still on a natural high by the news.

"You gonna love working for Endz!"

"You call him Endz?" Dana knew that only people who are close to Endz call him that. Only his grandmother who raised him, Momma Flo, called him Nicky.

"I'm married to his cousin, Miles," Dominique said.

"You got married."

"Yes, girl. Three years," Dominique waved her left hand showing off the fat rock Miles put on her finger. "It's Dominique Scott-Cooper now," she corrected. Dominique is the Quality Assurance Manager and Miles is the Production Manager. They went on to update each other. Dana shared how she was connected to Endz and glowed about her pregnancy. Dominique couldn't wait to be the godmother.

"So, we're gonna be working together. Just like old times," Dominique put her arm around Dana.

"I love the sound of that," Dana said.

As Dominique and Dana were talking, a six-foot-one, twenty-eight-year-old, chestnut skin toned, handsome man handed Dominique a glass of champagne. "Here you go, baby."

"Thanks. Dana, this is my husband, Miles Cooper. Miles, this is Dana. My homegirl from ASU," Dominique introduced.

"It's nice to finally meet you." Miles gave Dana a friendly hug. "The way Dominique talks about you it seems like we're old friends."

Approaching the group was a five-foot, full-figured, espresso skin toned, young woman who slightly resembled Dominique. With her was a five-foot-three, golden bronzed skin, slim thick, young woman in tow.

"Dominique, this party is great," the full-figured young woman said.

"Thank you for inviting us," Golden bronze said.

"Anytime girls," Dominique said. "Dana, do you remember my baby sister, Patresha Glover?" She pointed at the full-figured

20

young woman.

"You're Patresha? Man, how time flies." Dana hugged her. "How old are you now?"

"Eighteen and this is my best friend Lexus. She's nineteen." Patresha pointed to her golden bronze friend.

"They're both freshmen at ASU and roommates," Dominique said.

"Yeah whatever," Miles playfully scoffed.

"Fort Valley State Alum," Dominique whispered to Dana, Lexus, and Patresha to explain Miles' attitude towards their alma mater.

"Oh!" they all exclaimed with understanding and giggled amongst themselves.

"Being a hater ain't sexy, baby," Dominique teased Miles and gave him a kiss.

"What's going on here?" Neil appeared out of nowhere wanting to know who these people were that Dana was talking to. With his controlling jealous insecure ass.

Dana went on to make the introduction. "Everyone this is my fiancé, Neil. Baby, this is my best friend, Dominique, and her husband, Miles. He's Endz's cousin."

"Hi!" Dominique and Miles greeted.

"And this is Dominique's sister, Patresha, and her friend, Lexus. They're students at ASU," Dana finished the introduction.

"Nice to meet you," Patresha and Lexus said.

"Nice to meet you too," Neil greeted back.

"I brought them to the party as a good learning experience to learn how to network," Dominique said.

"Too bad Wyatt couldn't make it," Lexus said with slight gloom.

"Who is Wyatt?" Neil asked.

"He's my boyfriend," Lexus answered. "He goes to ASU too. He had to work. He's a part-time security guard and he's filling in for a coworker tonight."

"Nice young man," Miles said about Wyatt.

"His ass better be!" Dominique declared. "I'd kill for my baby sister." She pulled Patresha in with one of her arms. "Both of them." She pulled Lexus close to her with her other arm. She glanced over at Dana and took her by the hand. "Well three of them."

Endz came up to them and gave Miles a manly hug. "Hey, lil cuz. You enjoying yourself?"

"Yes man," Miles said.

"Good. Neil, can I holla at you for a second?" Endz motioned for Neil with his index finger to follow him to a secluded part of the room.

"What's up?" Neil asked.

"Dana is a wonderful and special lady," Endz said. "You are the luckiest man in the world. That girl is my people and you take good care of my people."

"I will," Neil said.

"Good because not so pretty things happen to motherfuckers who fuck with my people," Endz said with harshness in his voice. He then switched back to his charming debonair powerful demeanor. "You enjoy yourself and good luck." Endz left Neil alone with his thoughts.

Chapter 3

"Did y'all have a good time at the party?" Miles asked Patresha and Lexus who was sitting in the backseat of his champagne-colored Cadillac Escalade.

"Yes, we did," Patresha answered.

"It was nice of Mr. Washington to give us internships," Lexus said.

"Nice nothing. Y'all earned them shits," Dominique turned around in her passenger seat and said. "You two are bright young ladies and future successful businesswomen."

"Thank you," Lexus said. "You hear that Patresha! We're gonna be businesswomen!" She glanced over at her friend and noticed her smiling and giggling as she sent text messages on her phone. "Who you texting?" Lexus asked to be nosy.

"Oh, a new friend I met at the party." Patresha blushed.

"Ooooh! Whoever this friend is they having you smiling from ear to ear," Miles noted.

"I know his ass better treat my baby sister right," Dominique is very protective of Patresha. She's been through so much in her young life. She's self-conscious about her weight and not had the best experiences with men. Dominique was thankful for Lexus. She was the only friend in Patresha's life that's been genuinely loyal to her. In fact, Lexus reminded Dominique of herself in her younger years.

"Here we are!" Miles parked in front of Patresha and Lexus's on-campus apartment complex. "Y'all stay safe and goodnight."

"Goodnight," Patresha and Lexus said as they get out of the vehicle.

All of the sudden a navy-blue Chrysler 300 parked beside Miles vehicle. A twenty-one-year-old, six foot two, handsome, muscular, milk chocolate skinned young man with a neatly trimmed mini afro looking sexy in his security guard uniform with his last name Edwards shown on his nametag stepped out of the car and approached Lexus. He pulled her into a tight embrace and gave her a kiss on the lips and stroked her long curly light brown hair he loved so much. "Hi, baby."

"Hey, Wyatt," Lexus greeted her man. "How was work?"

"It was okay," Wyatt answered. He glanced over at Patresha, Miles, and Dominique who were still in the car. "Hey everybody."

"Hey Wyatt," they all greeted the respectable hardworking young man.

"Let me walk y'all back to the apartment," Wyatt offered Lexus and Patresha and they were on their way inside the building.

*****

"That was a great party," Miles said to Dominique on their way home.

"Yes, it was," Dominique cheerfully agreed. "I'm so happy to run into Dana. I got my homegirl back!" Then suddenly she went into deep thought.

"That's great, baby." Miles looked over at his beautiful wife wondering what she was thinking about. He could tell whatever it was had her concerned. "But..."

"But what?"

"I see that look on your face," Miles pointed out. "That look on your face says you are thinking and worried about something."

"Alright, you got me," Dominique confessed. "It's Dana's fiancé."

Miles raised his eyebrow. "What about him?"

"Something about him doesn't sit right with me. I think he's hiding something or not treating Dana right," Dominique voiced her concerns.

"You are good at reading people, but let's not jump to conclusions yet. If he is up to no good, it'll come out sooner or later. It always does," Miles said.

"You're right about that," Dominique leaned over to kiss Miles on the cheek. "I'm so lucky to have a loyal husband like you."

"I love you, baby." Miles held Dominique's hand. "I would never do anything to hurt you."

"I know."

"And I'm not trying to have us end up on an episode of *Snapped*," Miles added and the two busted out with hysterical laughter.

"You got that shit right."

Miles wasn't stupid. He knows Dominique doesn't play about her family, her people, her money, and her marriage. He knows if he even thought about cheating on Dominique or doing her dirty in any way all hell would break loose. That's why for Neil's sake his ass better be on his best behavior because he had no idea how he and his big cousin Endz get down.

Jamila

Chapter 4

It was Dana's first day at her new job. She loved her office which was in a building in downtown Albany, Georgia. She loved her new position. This was the first time in a long time she felt like her old self again. She felt like a real boss sitting behind her desk hard at work on her computer.

Knock! Knock!

"Come in!" she shouted. She looked up and saw Neil with a picnic basket. "Hey, Neil! What brings you by?"

"I wanted to bring your lunch to celebrate your first day at your new job," Neil answered and placed the picnic basket on the table.

"Thank you so much." Dana got out of her chair to walk over to Neil, giving him a hug and kiss. They sat on the couch to enjoy their lunch which consisted of lasagna and bottled water.

"When is your next doctor's appointment?" Neil asked between bites. "I want to be there."

"It's tomorrow morning at nine," Dana answered and took a sip of her water. "I really appreciate that."

When the engaged couple finished their meal, Neil said. "I better head back to work." The two got off the couch.

"Alright. Thanks for lunch." Dana kissed Neil.

They continued to kiss until Lexus, Patresha and Wyatt entered the office. "Oh, pardon us." Lexus blushed with embarrassment.

"Oh, y'all come on in here. It's cool!" Dana stopped the kiss and welcomed the young adults into her office. "Neil, you remember Lexus and Patresha from the party?"

"Oh, yes. Hi ladies," Neil said as he gathered the trash from the lunch and put it inside the picnic basket.

"These girls are interns," Dana said. "How's it going ladies?"

"Great!" Lexus handed Dana a folder. "Here's the file you requested, Ms. Dana."

"Thanks, Lexus." Dana grabbed the folder and placed it on

her desk.

"Excuse my manners, Ms. Dana. This is my boyfriend, Wyatt. Wyatt this is Ms. Dana and her fiancé, Neil," Lexus introduced.

"Nice to meet y'all," Wyatt said. He then glanced over at Neil and took a good look at his face. "Say you look familiar. Have we met?"

"I don't think so." Neil shook his head.

Wyatt brushed it off figuring if he had seen Neil before it'll come to him eventually. He then turned to his lovely lady and her homegirl. "Alright, I'm here to pick y'all up."

"We'll be finished in about fifteen minutes," Lexus said to Wyatt. He took his leave and waited in the lobby.

Dana glanced over and noticed the bouquet of flowers in Patresha's hand. "Patresha, who gave you those flowers? They're beautiful!"

"Her mystery man!" Lexus teased.

"Oh, stop it, Lexus!" Patresha gave her a playful shove.

"Well, he is! When are we gonna meet this guy?" Lexus asked curiously.

"Those flowers are beautiful!" Dana reiterated. "Bright red tulips. Neil gave me these exact same flowers."

"Yeah, that's right." Really, Neil didn't remember. He just picked some random flowers to get his foot in the door to snag Dana.

"When we first met," Dana reminded and decided to share the story with the two young ladies. "I was working at the main post office on Slappy Boulevard. Neil came in and was all pissed because his package from Amazon was two days late."

"Yeah, I was pissed as fuck," Neil added to the story. "But when I saw this beautiful face smile at me as she walked towards me, I calmed down." He wrapped his arms around Dana. "And when her sexy voice said, 'I was told about your issue and I deeply apologize. I'll do whatever I can to resolve your issue,' I completely forgot why I was pissed."

"She made it hard to stay pissed." Neil smiled. "I felt a little better. Even if they never found my package, I would've been cool with that."

"Did they find your package?" Lexus asked.

"Yes, they did," Neil answered. "I came back the next day with a bouquet of flowers thanking Dana and asked her out to dinner. And the rest is history."

"Right." Dana rubbed her stomach where her baby was growing and resting comfortably. "And the story is still being written."

Jamila

Chapter 5

"Oh shit! Oooh!" The sounds of Patresha's pleasure-filled moans echoed throughout the on-campus apartment she shared with Lexus. "Oh yes! Yes!" Patresha moaned out with sexual ecstasy.

"What the hell?" Lexus yawned out as she awakens from her deep slumber. She heard Patresha moan again and instead of being pissed, she let out a chuckle. "You go, girl! Get it, girl!"

"Oh shit! Aaah!" Patresha's moaning grew louder.

"Whoever that nigga is needs to hurry up and nut so I can go back to sleep," Wyatt complained in his half-sleep laying next to Lexus.

"Oh Wyatt, let her have her fun. Hating ain't sexy." Lexus giggled.

"What the fuck ever." Wyatt sat up rubbing his eyes and yawned.

"Besides it's only fair. I'm pretty sure we kept her up a while ago." Lexus' pussy was still sore from the pounding Wyatt gave her with his thick, curved, nine-inch dick.

Wyatt cracked a smile about how good Lexus' pussy felt nutting all over his dick. "Oh, that was different." He wrapped his arms around Lexus and gave her voluptuous titties a squeeze.

"Nigga, you a mess." Lexus hugged and kissed Wyatt and rested in his arms until the sounds of Patresha's moaning stopped. "I guess they're done." She assumed. "I'm gotta go to the bathroom."

Lexus climbed out of bed and found Wyatt's black t-shirt on the floor. *All that ass!* Wyatt thought as he admired Lexus' plumped backside before she slipped on his t-shirt to cover her nude body.

"Baby, can you grab me a bottle of water on your way back?"

"You got it." Lexus leaned in to kiss Wyatt before leaving her room.

Lexus went into the bathroom to urinate and wash her hands. Then she walked into the kitchen to grab the two water bottles in the refrigerator. She closed the refrigerator door and turned around and saw a man leaving Patresha's room and heading for the door. Lexus saw the man's face and was in complete shock.

"What the fuck!?" Lexus didn't mean to say it out loud, but it just came out.

The man turned around to see who said it. He saw Lexus standing there and correctly assumed it was her. He smiled, blew a kiss at her, and said, "Goodnight, sexy beauty," in an unwelcomed manner and walked out.

Lexus was freaked the fuck out. She rushed to the door and locked it. She couldn't believe what she just discovered. She didn't know what to do. Her only option was to talk to Patresha and ask her what the fuck was going on. She went into Patresha's room and let herself in without bothering to knock first. She turned on the lights and closed the door behind her.

"Patresha, what the hell?" Lexus needed to get to the bottom of this shit.

Patresha sat up. "I'm sorry. I guess I was too loud."

"I'm not talking about that. Is he the nigga you seeing?" Lexus already knew the answer. She just wanted to see what Patresha was gonna say.

"You can't tell anybody," Patresha said. "We want to keep our relationship private."

"You mean he wants to keep y'all relationship private," Lexus corrected. "Of course, he wants to keep it private. That nigga is engaged to Ms. Dana and they have a baby on the way! Not to mention Ms. Dana is your sister's friend."

"He's breaking up with her," Patresha said hopefully.

She can't be this gullible! Lexus thought with pity. "Please tell me you didn't buy his bullshit?"

"He is!" Patresha insisted. "He says she doesn't treat him right and the baby ain't even his."

"Come on. What nigga gonna stay with a woman who cheated on him and got pregnant by another nigga? If that was true, he would've been broke up with her," Lexus tried to talk some sense into Patresha. "That nigga is using you. You need to end this and end it now!"

"He's the only man that's been good to me," Patresha said with sadness. "He says he loves me."

Lexus sat next to Patresha on the bed. "Look, I know you had bad experiences when it comes to love, but this ain't love. He's using you." She tried to talk some sense into her desperate, low self-esteem having, best friend. "Let me ask you this. Has he taken you out on a date? Did he ever ask you about yourself? Did he introduce you to his people?"

Patresha's silence and shame on her face told Lexus everything she needed to know. "That nigga is no good. Please stay the fuck away from him or else he's gonna drag you down so far that you will never get back up. You deserve so much better than that nigga. Think about what I said." Lexus hugged Patresha and left her room.

Lexus knew Patresha was not gonna listen to her. She was definitely not gonna tell Patresha what Neil said and did before he left. She knew Patresha would never believe her. Even if Patresha did believe her, Lexus knew Neil would give Patresha some bullshit lie. And unfortunately, she would believe every word of it and accept his fake ass apology.

Lexus went back to her room and closed the door behind her. She saw Wyatt standing in the middle of the room in his black boxers with a stern look on his face.

"Wyatt, what's wrong?" Lexus asked and gave him a water bottle.

"Why the fuck was that nigga here? I saw his ass leave when I looked out the window." Wyatt opened the water bottle and took a sip. "That nigga is bad news." He was dead serious.

"I know." Lexus started drinking her water. "Hopefully, Patresha listened to me and leave his ass alone." She didn't dare tell Wyatt what Neil pulled on her. Wyatt would've beat Neil's ass. Or worse. Kill his nasty ass.

"You don't know that half of it."

Lexus gave Wyatt a crazy look. "What are you talking about?"

"I finally figured out where I seen that nigga before," Wyatt said and the two took a seat on the bed.

"Where?" Lexus asked.

Wyatt began to explain. "It was my first night doing security. I was at the club and that nigga was all up on some girl. Kissing her and touching all over her body and shit. Then this woman came in and got in his face. I think it was his girlfriend at the time. The nigga pulled his girlfriend out of the club and started yelling in her face. He was about to slap her, but one of the guards stopped him and threw him out. The security guard escorted the girlfriend to her car, making sure she got in safely. Before he left he yelled out to her 'your ass better be at the wedding tomorrow' those exact words."

After hearing Wyatt's story, Lexus' feelings went from deep concern to quivering fear. "I hope he's not hitting Ms. Dana. She's cool and she's pregnant."

"I don't think he's low enough to hit a pregnant woman," Wyatt said.

"Let's hope not," Lexus said. "In the meantime, let's hope that Patresha came to her senses and cut that nigga off." *But I know she's not gonna do it.*

Chapter 6

"Neil baby! I'm on my way home! The business trip ended earlier than scheduled. I'll tell you all about it when I see you. I love you. Bye!" Dana hung up the phone after leaving a voicemail message on Neil's phone as she drove home from the airport in her chrome BMW.

She was coming home from a two-week business trip to Los Angeles and San Francisco. Dana loved her job. She missed being a career woman. Also, she loved reconnecting with her girl, Dominique. Things between her and Neil are going great and back to being just like the beginning of their relationship. Now they're focused on becoming parents soon.

Dana arrived at the house and parked her car in the driveway. She rubbed her now showing pregnant belly. "I can't wait 'til you show up." Dana got out of the car and went inside the house.

"Baby, I'm home!" Dana announced herself.

Neil appeared downstairs in his swim trunks and Dana walked over to hug and kiss her fiancé. "Oh, Neil! I missed you so much!"

"What are you doing back so early?" Neil was not expecting Dana to come home, his facial expression and demeanor showed it.

"Didn't you get my message? The trip ended early."

Before Neil could say anything, a brown-skinned woman wearing jet black bundles in a white string bikini showing off her thick and shapely, five-foot-three body with a glowing smile on her beautiful face walking through the patio doors where the pool was located. "Neil baby! What's taking so long? I wanna fuck in the pool again!" she said as she approached him.

"Darnella!" Dana knew exactly who this thot was. This is the hoe who Neil cheated with and the bitch caused her to get suspended from her job at the post office.

Darnella looked at Dana up and down. "Oh, your ass again." Her eyes zeroed in on Dana's pregnant belly. "No wonder Neil came back to me. I see you let yourself go."

"Get the fuck out my house, hoe!" Dana snapped at Darnella.

"Whatever, bitch!" Darnella rolled her eyes and waved Dana off like she was a peon. "I'm going back to the pool." And turned around to head outside on the patio.

No, this hoe didn't! Dana was not gonna be disrespected in her own home. Especially by the likes of a shameless thot like Darnella. Dana ran out to the patio to handle her business.

"Dana get your ass back here!" Neil ordered but it was pointless. Dana didn't even hear him. Her only focus was to drag this bitch. When Dana got close enough, she jumped on Darnella's back and started punching her in the head and the back of her neck.

"Get the fuck off me you crazy bitch!" Darnella screamed with pain and the ladies fell to the ground. Dana was still on top of Darnella punching her in the face and chest.

"I told your hoe ass to get the fuck out!" Dana screamed and gave Darnella's face another punch.

"Dana get off her." Neil started to pull Dana off Darnella. "You're pregnant!"

"After I'm finished tearing this bitch up!" Dana continued to beat the shit out of Darnella until Neil finally managed to completely pull Dana off Darnella. He turned to Darnella and said, "Just get dressed and wait outside. I'm gonna take you home."

Dana snatched away from Neil and yelled, "You ain't taking this bitch no motherfucking where! Her hoe ass know how to get a motherfucking Uber!" She then turned to Darnella with a look of pure hatred on her face. "Get the fuck out!"

Darnella grabbed her clothes and ran off. Dana was struggling to catch her breath. Neil grabbed her tightly and shook her. "Get a hold of yourself!"

Dana pushed Neil away from her and slapped the shit out of him. "Get a hold of myself? You're cheating on me with that Darnella bitch again!" Dana thought she saw the last of that bitch. The nerve of this nigga bringing her ass up in their house. "You said you were done with her ass!"

"Look, it just happened!" Neil yelled in Dana's face. "Face it! You just can't fuck worth a shit! And your head game is straight fucking trash!"

Those words hurt Dana deeply. They hurt worse than all the ass beatings she was ever subjected to by this bastard altogether. She was not gonna let Neil get away with this disrespectful bullshit. Not this motherfucking time.

"Well excuse me for not having the skills of a porn star like that ran through thot's pussy you love so much," Dana shot back. "I'm sorry I loved you so much to the point that I gave you my virginity and you're the only man on the list, but don't worry. That'll change. Two can play this game. I hear niggas love pregnant pussy." Dana flashed a victorious evil smirked and turned to walk away like a boss.

Neil couldn't believe what the fuck Dana had the nerve to say to his face. He hated that shit. He was losing control over Dana. The thought of Dana fucking another nigga, especially with his seed growing inside of her. *Nasty, filthy, little bitch ass hoe!* Neil ran full speed and pushed Dana into the pool.

"Oh shit!" Dana yelled out before her body hit the water.

Neil dived headfirst into the pool. He pulled Dana by her hair and started dunking her head in the water.

"Neil!" Dana cried out as she struggled to get her head from under the water, but Neil kept dunking her head. "Stop!"

"Talk that shit now, bitch!" Neil yelled with fury as he dunked Dana's head in the water as she struggled. "You wanna be a hoe!" He dunked her head again.

"Neil!" Dana struggled to get free, but Neil overpowered her and held her head down. She continued to struggle until she ran out of strength and became motionless.

Neil let her go and got out of the pool. He glanced over at Dana who was still face down in the pool. "And stay your fucking ass in here!" He evilly spat out before leaving to take Darnella home and possibly put in another round or two of fucking. Neil slammed the door behind him.

Darnella was sitting on the porch waiting patiently for Neil. He pulled her out of her seat and kissed her. "Sorry about that baby," he apologized. The two hopped into his car and left.

In the pool, out of nowhere, Dana burst out from underwater like she was Ariel from *The Little Mermaid*. The only difference was Dana was a mermaid filled with rage. "Bitch! You son of a bitch! Fuck this shit!" Dana climbed out of the pool. She entered the house and marched upstairs and into the bedroom. She took off her wet clothes, changing into some sweatpants and a t-shirt. She put her wet hair into a ponytail.

She grabbed a few bags and packed everything she could. She knew Neil would be gone for a while because knowing his trifling ass, he'll probably be in Darnella's guts the second they get inside the dirty little slut's house. Normally, no woman wants to be cheated on. However, in Dana's case, this time Neil's cheating gave her plenty of time to pack her shit and leave before he comes back which would probably be when the sun is out.

After packing her bags, Dana carried and dragged them downstairs. She opened the door and exited the house. She put her bags in the trunk, hopped in the car, and took off as fast as she could.

As Dana was driving, she realized she had no idea where she could go. Ant lived in Atlanta. She didn't wanna impose on Dominique and Miles. Plus, she didn't wanna reveal the truth about her relationship with Neil. Dana knew who she could call and would help her out. No questions asked. She made the call.

"What's up?" Endz greeted.

Dana had to do this without sounding like she was in distress or despair. Neil's ass better be lucky because if Eli was alive and got word of how Neil was abusing his baby sister, he would've never seen the light of day again. And Endz would've taken care of Neil on Eli's behalf. As far as Dana was concerned, she was doing Neil's ass a favor. Something his abusive punk-ass does not deserve.

"Endz, do you mind if I stay with you for a while? I need to clear my head," Dana asked being half truthful.

"Of course," Endz said. "I'll wait up for you."

"Thanks. I'm on my way," Dana said before ending the call and headed straight for her safe haven.

Jamila

Chapter 7

Dana made great use of Endz' home office to do her work on her laptop at his desk while he was at the office. She decided to work from home for three weeks or until Neil got the hint that she didn't wanna be bothered with him. Whichever came first. She didn't wanna face him. She knew her office downtown would be the first place he would go to find her, and she didn't want any embarrassing scenes at her place of employment...again.

Ring! Ring!

Dana picked up the phone to answer without checking the caller ID first. "Hello!"

"Where the fuck you at?" Neil yelled into the phone.

"Well good morning to you too, Neil," Dana replied with sarcasm. "I guess you forgot I used to be a lifeguard," she pointed out her ability to hold her breath underwater for a long period of time while Neil was trying to drown her in the pool.

"Get your motherfucking ass home right now!"

"You can forget that after you cheated on me with that hoe. The same hoe that embarrassed me at the post office and got me suspended. I was too ashamed to come back to work. Then throwing my inexperience with sex in my face, and you tried to drown me!" Dana stood her ground.

"Look, I'm sorry! Now come back home!" Neil demanded. "I know your ass ain't in your office because I just checked!"

I was right! His controlling ass did check my office! Dana thought correctly.

If Neil thought a meaningless apology was enough for Dana to come back, he was dead ass wrong. Dana looked at the clock on the wall to see what time it was to confirm Neil was full of shit. "It's past noon and you're just now calling me trying to see where the fuck I am? I guess that hoe's pussy kept you up all night and you're just now getting to the house."

"It's none of your motherfucking business where the fuck I've been!"

"Then it's none of your motherfucking business where the

fuck I'm at!" Dana retorted.

"Dana, I ain't playing with your ass. Where the fuck are you?" Neil was losing his patience, but Dana didn't give a fuck.

"My location is not important. What is important is that I'm tired of your lying, abusive, community dick having, fuck boy ways and I'm not stepping one foot in that house until you start acting like you have some damn sense. Goodbye!"

Dana hung up before Neil could spew out any more of his threatening nonsense. Dana shook her head as she thought back to her first encounter with Darnella which caused her suspension from the post office which led to the first time Neil put his hands on her.

*****

Fourteen Months Earlier

Dana was in great spirits. She was doing great for a recent college graduate. She was loving her job at the post office. She might make a career out of it. If not, she had so many other options at her disposal. Like moving to Atlanta, Georgia to help with her beloved sister-in-law, Ant's, business. Also, she was on the arm of one of the sexiest, charming, and successful bachelors in Georgia. Neil was an amazing man to Dana. She never dreamed of being in a relationship with a man like him.

She was on her way back to work from her lunch break at Cheddar's in her chrome BMW that belonged to her deceased big brother, Eli. She loved that car. Neil offered to buy her a new car, but she declined. This car was Eli's. This car was filled with fond memories she shared with Eli and she wanted to hang onto those memories.

Dana arrived at the post office and made her way inside to the back where the break room was located.

"I'm back! I'm back! I'm back! I'm back! I'm back!" Dana rapped as she made her entrance.

"What's up, girl?" Marcie, Dana's co-worker, greeted. She

was a beautiful Puerto Rican with her long, curly, black hair in a ponytail.

Mr. Watson, who was also the manager entered the break room with an envelope in his hand. He was a tall and muscular, dark-skinned, older black man who was a retired Desert Storm Army Veteran. "Hey Dana, while you were gone somebody left this for you." He handed her the envelope.

"For real? Who?" Dana asked.

"I don't know. Some dude," Mr. Watson said and took his leave.

"It's probably from my man, Neil." Dana assumed with a schoolgirl giggle. "He's so sweet. Leaving me little notes. How sweet."

"Yeah! Yeah! Yeah!" Marcie teased.

"Oh, stop hating." Dana took a closer look at the envelope and noticed something strange. Her name was written with unique penmanship. Nothing she's ever seen before. "This ain't Neil's handwriting," Dana said and opened the envelope to read the message:

Dana, you are a beautiful, sweet, and special young lady. You deserve better.

Yours truly,

A concerned friend

"Anything wrong?" Marcie noticed the puzzled look on Dana's face.

"No, I'm good." Dana shook her head. She stuffed the note back in the envelope and put it in her handbag. "It's nothing."

"Alright," Marcie said. "By the way, it's your turn to be at the register,"

"I thought Sally was at the register," Dana said as she clocked back in on the computer from her break.

"Yeah, but she left early and you're next up."

"Okay." Dana shrugged.

"I'll be right there to join you in a minute," Marcie said.

"Okay," Dana said and went to take over the register. So far it was the usual. Mailing packages, letters, printing out money orders, certified letters, post office boxes, passports purchases. The post office wasn't very crowded today, so it was all good. Especially since Marcie joined Dana up front which helped speed things up a little.

After Dana mailed a package to New York for a lady, she was available for the next customer since Marcie was stuck with a customer who needed five money orders, five certified letters, and needed to make an appointment to obtain a passport.

"I can help the next person," Dana announced, and a beautiful young woman approached her register.

"Hello, may I help you?" Dana did her usual professional customer service greeting. The woman didn't say anything. She just started at Dana in silence. Dana found this odd. Maybe she didn't hear me? She guessed. "Ma'am, is there anything I can do for you?" she asked the question again but a little bit louder.

"Yeah," the woman finally spoke. "Stay the fuck away from my man, bitch!" she snapped.

Dana looked around like who the fuck was this bitch talking to. Marcie looked over like she was ready to jump to Dana's defense, but Dana gave her a non-verbal signal letting her know that she got this. She turned back to the woman and asked while trying to maintain her professionalism, "I beg your pardon?"

"You heard me, bitch!" the woman yelled. "You've been fucking my nigga, Neil, for almost a damn year and I'm tired of this shit!"

Dana was getting pissed and humiliated. Why the fuck was this bitch coming for her in her place of employment with this bullshit? In fact, how in the fuck did she know where she worked and who her man is?

There was only one customer remaining in line, a woman with her kids. She turned and walked out as soon as the drama unfolded. She didn't want her kids to witness the display.

However, if she was by herself, she would've stayed for the show. So, it was just Dana, Marcie, and the bitch.

Dana had a lot of questions, but she wasn't gonna ask this ghetto, ratchet, hoodrat shit. She'll save those questions for Neil when she gets off work, but for now, she had to keep up her professional demeanor because she was still on the clock.

"Uh... I have no idea what you're talking about. I'm in a relationship with a man named Neil. You must be mistaken for another man named Neil." The bitch was about to say something else, but Dana cut her off. "I'm sorry, but if you don't have any business that is post office related that I can assist you with, I'm afraid I'll have to ask you to leave."

Dana turned around and walked away as Marcie followed her. Dana was shaking. She couldn't possibly continue to work after what just transpired. "Marcie, can you handle the front by yourself for a while until I get myself together?"

"Dana watch out!" Marcie screamed.

Dana felt something push her to the floor. She tried to get up but was kicked in the stomach. "Stuck up ass bitch!" Somehow the woman was able to leap over the counter to get to Dana.

At that moment, the professional shit flew right out the motherfucking window. Dana hopped on her feet and punched that hoe in the jaw. She grabbed her by her hair and punched her face five times.

"Let me go, bitch!"

"Crazy ass bitch!" The women exchanged blows, tumbled on the floor scratching and kicking each other.

"Dana that's enough!" Marcie tried to pull Dana off the woman but to no avail.

"No, it ain't!" Dana yelled and gave the woman another punch in the eye.

Marcie still struggled to pull the ladies apart and Mr. Watson came to help Marcie pull the women apart. Unlike Marcie, Mr. Watson had the strength to break up a fight. He turned to the woman and yelled, "Whoever the fuck you are, get your ass out of here!"

"This ain't over, Dana! Believe that shit!" the woman threatened and left the same way she came, by jumping over the counter and stomping out the door.

How does this bitch know my name? *Dana thought.*

After everybody calmed down, Mr. Watson gave his instructions. "Marcie take over the front. Dana come into my office."

Marcie went on to the register, Dana followed Mr. Watson into his office and closed the door behind them.

"Mr. Watson, I can explain. That was self-defense," Dana pleaded her case.

"I know. I understand," Mr. Watson said and sat at his desk. "I saw the whole thing and I know you. You are a hardworking and dignified young lady. I saw you tried to handle the situation as professionally as you could."

"Thank you."

Mr. Watson sighed. "However, you do know due to policy I have to suspend you."

Dana was upset about the news, but she understood and accepted it. She was grateful that she didn't get fired. "I understand. You gotta do what you gotta do."

"Due to the circumstances, here's what I'll do. It'll be suspension with pay and when the suspension is over, I'll expunge it. It'll be like it never happened," Mr. Watson said.

"Thank you, sir." Dana shook Mr. Watson's hand. "I'll get my things. Goodbye."

"Goodbye and your suspension will be for the rest of the week. So, I'll see you next Monday."

Okay. *Dana turned to walk out but Mr. Watson stopped her. "Before you go, I need you to remember something. I need you to hear me and hear me good, okay? A real man would never dream of disrespecting his woman in any way and sure as hell would never allow another motherfucker to do it either. Keep that in mind."*

"Okay, Mr. Watson."

Dana walked out of the post office with shame and hopped in her car. She headed straight for Neil's house. She knew he'd be there because he didn't have to work today. On the way, she decided to call him. When she heard it pick up, she went ahead and blurted out, "Neil, I'm coming over right now because we need to talk."

"He's busy bitch!" a woman's voice answered and had the imaginary balls to say before hanging up in Dana's face.

Dana knew it was her. She knew it was the same bitch that came for her. "Now, I'm gonna kill this bitch!"

Dana arrived at Neil's house and used her key to get inside. She slammed the door behind her and saw Neil and the hoe on the couch. She was in the middle of sucking his dick. They both got up off the couch and put on their clothes.

"Baby let me explain," Neil had the nerve to say at a time like this.

"So, it is true? You are fucking this bitch! This hoe rolled up on me at the post office and got me suspended!" Dana had deep hurt in her heart.

"Suspended?" Neil asked with disbelief

"Yes!" Dana yelled. "She came there talking all types of shit about y'all and attacked me." She looked at the woman and added, "I guess she likes getting her ass beat." Dana referred to the fact that the hoe had the imaginary balls to still be in the house.

"Actually, I rather have my pussy beat by my nigga's long dick," the woman boasted with a smirk.

Whap!

Dana pimp slapped the hoe with her right hand. "Say that shit again, bitch!"

Whap!

Another pimp slap. This time with her left hand. "Huh!"

Punch!

"What you say?"

Punch!

"Talk hoe! Talk!"

Dana wanted to punch her again, but Neil managed to grab a hold of her and held her back. "Darnella get out!"

Darnella rubbed her cheek and walked towards the door. "I'll be back!"

"No, the fuck you won't!" Dana tried to lunge over to Darnella, but Neil's grasp was too strong. Plus, Darnella was already out the door.

Neil let Dana go and tried to explain himself, "Now Dana, listen."

"No, you listen to me, nigga!" Dana got in his face. "I ain't putting up with this shit! I loved you and gave you my all! You got bitches coming for me at my job and shit. Fuck this shit! It's over!"

Dana was deeply hurt. She loved this man with all her heart. So much so she gave him her virginity, and this is how he repaid her. There's no way she could stay with him after this.

Dana was headed for the door, but Neil grabbed her arm tight and pulled her towards him. "No, it ain't over!

Dana tried to pull away, but Neil's grip was too strong. "No motherfucker! It's over! I'm done! Enjoy your thot!"

"Look, your ass ain't going nowhere!" he ordered and threw her on the couch.

"Oh yes, the fuck I am!" Dana got off the couch. "Get the fuck out my way!"

"Sit the fuck down!'

"Fuck no!"

Whap!

Neil slapped Dana hard across the face, making her fall back on the couch. "I said sit your ass down!"

Dana held her face on the exact spot Neil slapped her. She couldn't believe it. He hit her. This nigga hit her. This nigga motherfucking hit her. This couldn't be the man she loved. A man who cheated on her and now put his hands on her.

"You put your hands on me? You put your hands on me?" Dana repeated. "Oh, it's really over now!"

Dana got up to leave again and Neil punched her in the face making her fall back on the couch. "Aaaah!" Dana screamed.

Neil pounced on top of her and put his hands around her

neck. "Shut the fuck up!"
Punch!
"It ain't over till I say it's over! You understand me bitch!"
"Neil stop!" Dana screamed as Neil held her down and started beating her.
"Shut the fuck up!"
"Help me! Somebody help me!"
Dana continued to struggle until she managed to kick Neil hard in the nut sack. She pushed him off her. While Neil was still on the floor grabbing his sore nuts, Dana grabbed her purse and keys and ran out of the house as fast as she could. She left vowing to never see Neil again.

*****

Dana really thought she was done with Neil forever. He called and texted her nonstop to apologize. Eventually, she gave in and gave him another chance. Her face was so fucked up from the beating. She was too ashamed to go back to work, so she quit her job at the post office. After she and Neil made up, he insisted that she moved in with him and she did.

Of course, the beating didn't stop. In fact, they got worse and Neil became bolder with his disrespect. He didn't want Dana to find another job and stay home to just take care of the house, especially now that she's pregnant.

Dana knew the only reason Neil allowed her to work for Endz was because saying no to one of the people who signs his checks would not be a good look. This was it. No more putting up with Neil's shit. Dana loved Neil. She wanted their future marriage and family to work and blossom. That's why she moved out to take drastic measures to change Neil. He's going to go back to being the nice, sweet charming gentleman that Dana fell in love with and she was gonna make sure of that.

Jamila

Chapter 8

After her shower, Lexus was in her lime green bathrobe in her room searching for the perfect outfit to wear to the club tonight while listening to "Carpet Burn" by DaBaby playing on her phone. This would be a great time to have a girls' night out since Wyatt was in Atlanta helping his brother and sister-in-law move into their new house. She found a beige-colored strapless dress to wear with some black stilettos.

Before getting dressed, she went into Patresha's room to see if she was ready to go. "Hey, girl! Let's go! We about to turn up in this motherfucking bitch!" Lexus cheered as she entered Patresha's room.

Lexus's mood changed when she found Patresha in distress on her phone. "Neil please call me! Where are you? I've been waiting for two hours!"

"What's the matter?" Lexus asked even though she already knew the answer.

Patresha wiped away her tears and pulled herself together enough to explain what was going on. "Neil was supposed to take me out to dinner, but he never showed up. He was supposed to pick me up two hours ago."

"I'm sorry to hear that," Lexus sympathized and took a seat next to Patresha and put her arm around her. "Look, fuck that nigga. His ass ain't shit anyway. Instead of sitting here wasting tears on a bitch ass fuck nigga, get in the shower, fix your hair and makeup, find a cute outfit to wear, and let's go out to dinner and then head to the club."

"Thank you for being my friend," Patresha said with a sniffle.

"Anytime! "You're sweet, good people and you are beauti-ful." *I just wished you knew that,* Lexus thought.

Patresha giggled a little bit. "What's so funny?" Lexus asked.

"I was just thinking back to our high school days," Patresha answered. "It's kind of crazy how we became friends in the first place."

Lexus joined in on the giggling. "Yes, it was."

******

It was Patresha's freshman year at Terrell County High School in Dawson, Georgia. She walked into the cafeteria and saw her boyfriend all up on another girl. She walked over to them to see what the fuck was going on. "Kenneth, what is going on?" she asked.

"What the fuck do you want?" Kenneth yelled at Patresha with venom in his voice as he pulled the other girl closer to him. "Can't you see I'm with my girl?"

The other girl kind of pulled away from Kenneth and asked. "What's going on?"

"It's nothing baby," Kenneth blatantly lied.

"I'm your girlfriend!" Patresha yelled with tears in her eyes. "You said you loved me!"

"It's over!" Kenneth coldly replied. "I got what the fuck I want. Now take your fat ass on somewhere. Just thinking about seeing your naked ass makes me wanna throw up!"

Patresha felt humiliated and used. She ran out of the cafeteria and into the girl's bathroom to cry her eyes out in a ball on the floor. While she was crying, someone gave her a tissue.

"Thank you." Patresha took the tissue to wipe her tears away. She looked up to see who gave her the tissue and was shocked to see it was the girl that Kenneth was all over.

"It's you!"

"Are you okay?" the girl asked with concern.

"No."

"Do you wanna talk about it?"

"Why are you being nice to me?" Patresha asked. "I thought you would still be in the cafeteria laughing at me with Kenneth."

"Please." The girl rolled her eyes and scoffed. "I just

dumped his ass. Well, first, I slapped the shit out of him. Then I dumped his ass. Now everybody is talking about him being slapped and dumped on the spot and forgot all about what he did to you."

"You broke up with him?"

"Yes, the fuck I did," the girl reiterated. "I don't fuck with niggas who disrespect females. That shit he pulled with you was foul as fuck. And if he did it to you, he will do it to me. In a way, you did me a favor by exposing his ass. What happened between you and Kenneth?"

The girl's kindness made Patresha feel like she could trust her enough to spill her guts. "He said he loved me. He said that if I loved him, I'd have sex with him and give him money. He didn't want to go public with our relationship because he didn't want people in our business."

That motherfucker! *The girl thought.* This nigga was a selfish, shallow, and evil user. His ass played on this sweet innocent girl's low self-esteem and insecurities about her body to manipulate and take advantage of her.

"Did you give him two hundred dollars yesterday?" the girl asked.

Patresha eyes widened with disbelief. "How did you know that?"

The girl sighed and reached into her purse. She took out a wad of cash and handed it to Patresha. "I think this belongs to you."

"Thank you." Patresha took her money back. This girl was truly amazing and sweet. She didn't have to return the money and she was being comforted without judgment.

"If you don't mind me asking. How did you get this money?" The girl was curious because that was a lot of money for a high school girl.

"My big sister Dominique sends me and my grandmother money every week," Patresha explained. "She has a good job, so she can afford to help us out with money. She is also dating a nice man that she works with who is rich. His name is Miles."

"That's good that she looks out for you." The girl nodded her head. "I have a big brother who is in the Army. He just got married. By the way, what's your name?"

"Patresha. What's yours?"

"Lexus."

"You're named after a luxury car?"

Lexus laughed. "That's what everybody calls me. My name is really Alexandria. You see, daddy wanted to name me after his dream car and momma wanted to name me after her favorite aunt who died of breast cancer."

"I get it," Patresha said. "So, they compromised. having Alexandria be your government name and Lexus be your nickname. I wish I was pretty like you," Patresha said with sadness.

"You are pretty," Lexus said. "Never let a nigga or bitch make you think differently."

"Thank you." Patresha hugged her new friend.

"Hey, you had my back. Now I have yours."

*****

"Can you believe that nigga got like five kids, behind on child support and living off his wife who is a Marine?" Patresha laughed at Kenneth's life update.

"I can believe it. Good thing we ain't in that bullshit." Lexus laughed.

"I know right!" Patresha laughed. "We dodged the fuck out of that bullet, didn't we?"

"Yes, the fuck we did!" Lexus exclaimed with relief. "I still can't believe Kenneth gave you the rest of your money back with interest and apologized. I wonder what made him come around?"

"Well, after our talk in the bathroom, I called Dominique and told her everything. The next day, she and Miles came to visit us. Miles asked what Kenneth's full name was and what he looked like, and I told him. After that, I didn't see him again until I came home from school the next day which was a few hours after I got that money back and an apology. I don't know what happened," Patresha's last statement didn't sound very convincing. Let's just say she and Lexus knew how Miles and his people rolled.

The young ladies burst out with hysterical laughter at the thought of Kenneth getting that well-deserved gangsta ass whooping.

"Can we go to IHOP before we hit the club? I'm starving!" Patresha asked.

"Girl me too," Lexus said. "Let's hurry up and get ready so we can eat and turn up!"

Jamila

Chapter 9

"It's popping in here tonight!" Lexus said as she and Patresha entered the club.

"Yes, it is!" Patresha said with amazement wearing her cute black and white jumpsuit with her arms out.

"Lexus! Patresha! Over here!" A six-foot light-skinned young man with a neatly trimmed beard with neatly freshly done cornrows braided all the way back motioned for the young ladies to join him at his table.

"It's Be-vo!" Patresha screamed out and she and Lexus spotted their twenty-one-year-old friend and classmate from their Political Science Class.

They went straight to his table and greeted simultaneously, "Hey Be-vo!"

"Hey ladies!" Be-vo hugged the ladies. "Let me get y'all something to drink. What y'all having?"

"Surprise us," Patresha answered.

"I got y'all," Be-vo said and headed for the bar.

"Dominique wants to take us shopping tomorrow," Patresha said to Lexus.

"Oh shit! I'm there!" Lexus never turns down a free shopping spree. "How do you think you did on that Biology test?"

"I think I aced it. I just hate this paper I gotta do."

"Please don't mention that paper to me right now!" Lexus shivered at the thought of that paper. "I might need to smoke a couple of blunts just thinking about it."

"Here are our drinks." Be-vo came back with the three drinks.

"Thanks," Lexus said.

"We appreciate you," Patresha said.

The ladies took a sip and loved the taste.

"These are great! What is it?" Patresha asked.

"Blue motherfuckers!" Be-vo blurted out.

"Lives up to the name." Lexus kept on sipping. "I might need three of these motherfuckers! Good thing we didn't take my car and got an Uber."

"I thought you were DJing tonight?" Patresha asked Be-vo. Be-vo's goal was to be the next DJ Khaled. If that doesn't work out, he could always become Dr. Bellamy Voce, Psychiatrist. Who knows? Maybe he'll take both career paths. The sky's the limit for him.

"Not tonight," Be-vo said. "But I got a gig tomorrow night. Y'all should come through."

Patresha wasn't sure if she was going. "I don't know..."

"We'll be there!" Lexus answered for both of them. "Hey, we have our whole lives ahead of us! Let's enjoy it!"

"You're right!" Patresha went along with the idea. "Be-vo, we'll be there!"

"Good!" Be-vo put his arms around Lexus and Patresha. "I knew I could count on my girls!" Lexus and Patresha reminded Be-vo of his little sisters back in his hometown of Tallahassee, Florida.

He always thought of them as his family away from home and wanted the best for them.

"I don't believe this shit!" Patresha was no longer in a festive mood.

"What's the problem?" Lexus asked.

Patresha didn't say anything. She just motioned her head to Neil in the corner who was all hugged up with another woman who was not Dana. *So that's why he stood me up!* Patresha's blood was boiling like lava.

"That motherfucker!" Lexus shared Patresha's anger.

"Who the fuck is that nigga?" Be-vo asked. He didn't know the nigga or what the fuck was going on, but he could tell already that Neil was a fuck nigga with absolutely no respect for women. Just by looking at his ass, he could figure that shit out. He had that natural gift of correctly reading people and being a psychology major helps too.

"It's a long and crazy story." Lexus shook her head. She didn't feel like giving a low-down nigga like Neil an ounce of her energy. "It's cool though. We're not gonna let fuck boys like him fuck up our good time," she dismissed and didn't give Neil a second thought.

"Good for y'all!" Be-vo congratulated.

"That's right!" Lexus laughed off. "Fuck that pussy ass nigga! Right Patresha?" Silence. Patresha didn't say anything. Lexus turned to her left where Patresha was sitting and didn't see her. "Patresha? Where did she go?"

"Oh shit! It's about to go down!" Be-vo saw Patresha walk up towards Neil and the woman.

"You're absolutely fucking right," Lexus said.

"Neil, what the fuck is going on?" Patresha rolled up on Neil and his female companion for the evening.

"Patresha, what the fuck do you want?" Neil yelled at her.

"You stood me up and I don't appreciate that shit!" Patresha was pissed off as fuck and she wanted this nigga to know how he made her feel.

"I really don't give a fuck what you appreciate," Neil snapped back.

Patresha glanced over at the woman who was smirking away. "Oh, don't show out in front of some random hoe you trying to stunt for!" Usually, Patresha wasn't this bold, but a few drinks in her system made her brave.

"Don't worry about what the fuck I'm doing or who the fuck I'm with!" Neil got in Patresha's face. "Take your fat ass on somewhere!"

Patresha was about to say something else, but the woman cut her off and got in her face. "You heard him you fat sloppy bitch! Get gone!" She pushed Patresha with great force to the ground causing her to stumble backwards and crashing into a table, knocking everything over.

Neil and the woman were laughing their shameless asses off at Patresha's humiliating expense causing some more people to join in on their cruel laughter. Patresha struggled to get up which caused the laughter to continue.

"Weak ass bitch!" the woman spat out as she and Neil cruelly enjoyed the spectacle. The two turned around to leave

Patresha to wallow in her humiliation.

"Where were we, baby?" Neil asked and gave the woman a kiss.

The woman was about to give her an answer and BOOM! She was hit in the back of the head with a champagne bottle by Lexus and fell to the ground. Lexus pounced on top of the woman, pulled her hair, and screamed in her face. "Nobody disrespects my homegirl like that bitch!" And then Lexus punched her in the face.

The ladies started to tussle all over the floor. Lexus was tearing that bitch's ass up. Lexus was not gonna stand idly by and let these motherfuckers dog her best friend out like that.

Neil was pissed. He saw Patresha still struggling to get off the floor. He yanked her off the floor and yelled with disgust. "You gonna pay for this you fat bitch!"

Neil was all set to pimp slap Patresha, but Be-vo stopped him in time by tackling him to the ground. "Oh, so you wanna hit a woman? Huh, nigga! Hit me instead, motherfucker!" Be-vo yelled as he gave Neil a right hook to the jaw.

The woman had her hands around Lexus' throat. Patresha ran over, kicked the woman in the ribs and stomach, so she could stop choking Lexus. Neil would've come to the woman's rescue, but Be-vo had him in the chokehold. Be-vo turned to his left and saw security running towards their way.

Be-vo threw Neil to the ground. "Oh, shit! Let's go!" He grabbed Lexus and Patresha by their hands and ran out of the club before they were caught. Even if they were caught it wouldn't have made a difference. Be-vo is cool with the owner and that's one of the spots Wyatt works security.

"We did it! We beat that bitch's ass!" Lexus high fived Patresha. "Girl, I'm so proud of you. The way you kept kicking that hoe! I'm so proud of you!" Lexus liked seeing this side of Patresha. She wished she showed it more often.

"You guys are a trip!" Be-vo laughed.

"Thanks, Be-vo for having my back." Patresha hugged Be-vo.

Into the Arms of His Boss

"Of course," Be-vo said. "I ain't letting a bitch ass nigga like that fuck with my people."

"I guess we got to get another Uber." Lexus pulled out her phone.

"Hey, there's another party on the west side of town I'm about to check out. Why don't y'all roll with me?" Be-vo suggested.

"Let's go!" Patresha cheered. "And I'm getting another blue motherfucker the second I get in that bitch!"

"There you go! We about to turn the fuck up!" Lexus cheered and she and Patresha followed Be-vo to his black Lincoln Navigator and climbed inside. Lexus and Patresha got in the back seat and Be-vo made himself comfortable in the driver's seat and drove off.

"Y'all are so crazy!" Be-vo laughed at the duo in the back backseat.

"Be-vo, you good," Patresha said with a giggle. "Now I know why they call it liquid courage."

"Maybe you need to drink blue motherfuckers more often," Lexus half-joked.

"Hey, Lexus! Look at this!" Patresha laughed at her phone and showed Lexus the text message she just received.

Neil: *You gonna pay for this you fat bitch!*

Patresha snickered at Lexus before sending a reply. "Watch this."

Patresha: *Nigga you can kiss my ENTIRE fat ass motherfucker! Fuck you and that bitch!*

"You go, girl!" Lexus was ecstatic to see Patresha stand up for herself and now that abusive and cheating ass fuck boy is out of her beautiful and sweet best friend's life forever.

Unaware that back at the club, Neil was all bruised up and sore standing around. He was pissed that Patresha came at him in

61

public like that and allowed her little friends to bitch him up like that. Oh no! He wasn't gonna stand for that shit. "I'm gonna get that little fat bitch!"

Chapter 10

After a long day at work, Dana went to the Albany Mall to find a present for Endz's grandmother, Florida Washington, for her birthday. She remembered Endz talking about a birthday dinner for her at the retirement home she lives at.

Dana went to Dillard's to the perfume counter to purchase a Chanel Chance perfume set. Dana thought Endz's grandmother would love it. It was her mother's favorite perfume. In fact, Dana thinks it was the only perfume she wore. After making her purchase, Dana had it gift wrapped and left the store.

She walked through the mall and headed for the food court. She had a craving for rocky road ice cream. She found the ice cream booth and made her way over when she heard a familiar voice mumble under her breath. "Fucking bitch!"

It was a mumble, but it was loud enough for Dana to hear which was the goal. Dana turned around and flashed a cocky smirk at her rival who was sitting at a table. "Oh, Darnella. It's great to see you." She greeted in a fake ass polite manner and approached Darnella's table.

Dana saw the minor cuts along Darnella's forehead. A black eye peeking out of her heavy makeup and due to her wearing a red halter top and short denim shorts, she was able to see marks all over her stomach. "Damn girl! You look like shit! If I didn't know any better, I'd think you got hit across the head with a champagne bottle. Punched in the face repeatedly, getting kicked in the stomach and ribs about three or four times," Dana correctly guessed the results of Darnella's altercation with Lexus, Patresha, and Be-vo.

"Well I'd love to stay and chat, but I have an event to attend and you're a shameless nasty ass whore." *Fuck that ice cream! Let me get away from this bitch!*

"You think you above everybody huh?" *Oh, I'm gonna wipe that smug look off this bitch's face. With the motherfucking truth!* Darnella thought. "Look at you acting like you the Queen Bee up in this bitch and you pregnant by a nigga who beats your ass and fuck other bitches."

"Who said I was with his ass now?" Dana asked without flinching. "I'm about to be Neil's wife and I'm carrying his child. We're just separated until we work out our issues. Not that it's any of your motherfucking business, but as a common courtesy I think I should let you know that ever since our separation he's been begging for me to come back to him and forgive him."

"Oh really? If he wanted your ass back why in the fuck was he all up on me at the club a few days ago?"

"And?" Dana asked as if she gave a fuck.

"And?" Darnella mocked Dana's 'I don't give a fuck' response. "While I was all up on Neil, some fat ass, low self-esteem having bitch rolled up on us talking all this shit about 'Neil why did you stand me up? Neil, why did you do me like that? Neil, I thought you loved me?' Boohoo motherfucking hoo!" She did Patresha's whining impersonation in order to mock her weak pathetic display. "Shit and I thought your ass was sad and pathetic." Darnella shook her head with pity.

Dana scoffed, but deep down she was pissed as fuck. However, she wasn't gonna show it. At least not in front of this bitch. "Well, who knows about being sad and pathetic better than you? And as far as that little, fat ass, low self-esteem having bitch is concerned." Dana took another look at Darnella's bruises. "She must not be too pathetic. Obviously, she fucked your ass up. I'm sure you provoked her by adding to her humiliation. I wish I could've been there to see that ass whooping. Well goodbye!"

Dana turned to walk away and went about her business giving zero fucks what else Darnella had to say. If Dana only knew if she did witness Darnella's ass whooping at the club and the events that led up to it, she would be done with Neil for good.

Chapter 11

On the outskirts of Albany, Georgia on the peaceful green lands of Dougherty County where the beautiful and luxurious Harmony Hills Retirement Home is located. There resides Florida Washington with the beauty and class of Diahann Carroll sprinkled with spice.

Momma Flo is what she's better known as had two beautiful daughters. Pearl, who was Endz's mother, and Ruby, who was Miles' mother. The family is originally from St. Louis, Missouri. Momma Flo was married to a man who was well respected in the community. He was a successful businessman and a powerful voice of black empowerment.

Things were great until scandal led to his downfall. It came out that he was having an affair with a white woman and had an outside child with her. As a result of the scandal, he was destroyed. He was disgraced. His business collapsed. Momma Flo did what was uncommon during those times when it came to these types of situations. She actually left and took the girls. They never saw him again and have no idea what became of him.

Momma Flo took the money from the divorce settlement, taking her girls to move in with her best friend who lived in Albany, Georgia, and started a new life. She ran a daycare center and became involved with programs that helped people in need. Women and children in particular. Momma Flo even opened up her own home for women and children to use as a safe haven.

In Momma Flo's home, she also raised Endz since he was orphaned at five years old. Miles was raised in Macon, Georgia, where his mother still lives alive and well, happily with Miles' stepfather, Oliver.

"Happy birthday, grandma!" Endz and Miles cheered on Momma Flo as they walked her into the dining room that was all decked out with birthday decorations with a seafood buffet and a table filled with gifts.

"Miles! Nicky!" Momma Flo kissed her handsome respectable grandsons on their cheeks. "This is wonderful! Thanks, my sweet and handsome grandbabies!"

"Hey, Momma Flo!" Dominique greeted and placed her gift on the table and walked over to hug her grandmother-in-law. "Sorry, I'm late. I got held up at the office. Happy Birthday!"

"Thanks, baby!" Momma Flo said.

Dominique walked over to Miles to hug and kiss him. "Hi, baby." She turned to face Momma Flo. "I just know you gonna love my gift."

"I know I will," Momma Flo said. "How's your sister doing?"

"She's good," Dominique answered. "I invited her to come, but she had a test to study for tomorrow. She sends her birthday wishes."

"Thank her for me and tell her to keep her nose in those books," Momma Flo stressed.

"Is there room for one more?" Dana asked as she walked in with her present and put it on the table. "I hope I'm not intruding."

"Girl get your ass over here and give me a hug! Talking all that shit about not wanting to intrude! Girl please!" Momma Flo pulled Dana into a tight hug.

"I missed you." Dana felt so much love and security in Momma Flo's arms.

"I miss you too, baby girl! How you been? Are you taking care of yourself and that baby?" Momma Flo rubbed Dana's pregnant belly.

"Yes ma'am." Dana smiles. "I can't wait for him or her to show up."

"I bet it's a her," Momma Flo guessed.

"Momma Flo, you always say that," Dominique laughed.

"Ain't it the truth," Miles said. "Now let's go eat." With that being said everybody went to get Momma Flo's dinner party ready. Dominique and Miles helped the chef with the birthday cake while Endz and Dana set the table.

"Thanks, Endz," Dana said to him.

"For what?" Endz asked.

"For everything. Giving me a job and letting me stay with you for a while." Dana was grateful to Endz. Letting her use his house as a safe haven.

"It's no problem," Endz insisted. "You are doing great things for the company. Also, I like having you around the house. It gets lonely living in that big house all by myself. It's hell sometimes, but I've gotten used to it."

Endz let out a little chuckle. "You know I'm so lonely I actually invited grandma to move in with me, but she refused."

"Really? Why?" Dana raised her eyebrow.

"She said she wanted her own space and didn't want her grandson cramping her style when she brings dates home."

Endz and Dana busted out laughing. "Your grandma is a trip!" Dana kept on laughing. She stopped laughing when she heard her phone ring. She took her phone out and saw it was Neil calling her. Hiding her frustration, she said to Endz. "I'm gonna step outside. I gotta take this."

"I'll be back everybody," Dana announced as she walked out the door and outside into the gardens.

Dana took a deep breath bracing herself for whatever bullshit Neil was on before answering the phone. "Hello."

"When the fuck are you coming home?" Neil angrily asked. He had enough of Dana's shit.

"Neil, I told you I'm not coming home until you stop putting your hands on me and sticking your dick in anything and everything that walks and breathes." Dana was not backing down. She was not only standing up for herself, but she's also standing up for her baby that's growing inside her.

"Dana, I'm sick of your motherfucking shit!"

What did this nigga just say? Dana was on pause. "You're sick of my what? You know what? I don't have time for this shit."

"I suggest you make time for this shit."

Dana was about to hang up on Neil's ass, but a thought came to her. Her mind flashed back to what went down before she came here and decided to address it. "You know I ran into Darnella at the mall earlier and she told me y'all was all up on each other at the club. She also told me that some other chick rolled up on y'all confronting you about standing her up. What was that about?"

"That's none of your motherfucking business!" Neil barked.

"Wrong answer." Dana hung up on Neil and went back to the party.

It was a great get-together. The food was amazing. Momma Flo loved the perfume Dana gave her and the black and white hat Dominique gave her. Momma Flo was looking forward to her birthday weekend trip to San Francisco, California with Ruby. Every year, Ruby takes Momma Flo on a trip on her birthday weekend to anywhere she wanna go. It was their special mother/daughter time together.

"Alright we're about to go in the entertainment room to watch movies," Endz said.

"What are we watching?" Dana asked.

"Yeah grandma, what are we watching?" Miles asked with Dominique on his arm.

"The *Irishman* and *Hustlers*," Momma Flo answered.

"You watch *Hustlers*?" Dana was surprised.

"Fuck yeah! Those bitches are wild!" Momma Flo cheered and they all took a seat in the entertainment room. Endz set up the television and the movie started playing. When the first movie was over, they went on to play the second movie.

"You know this is one of the best birthdays I've had in a long time," Momma Flo said. "I got my family and friends. The amazing presents. Don't get me started on the food. That shit was delicious."

Momma Flo looked over at Miles and Dominique cuddling. "Beautiful! Simply beautiful! Y'all keep each other happy!"

"We will grandma," Miles said and planted a kiss on Dominique's forehead. "I'm so happy I found my queen."

"And I'm happy I found my king," Dominique returned the kiss on Miles' lips.

"Nicky, when are you gonna get your queen?" Momma Flo asked Endz.

Endz shrugged. "I don't know grandma. I haven't found her yet."

"Oh yes, you have," Momma Flo pointed out. "You just haven't figured it out yet."

"What is she talking about?" Dana asked Endz.

"Beats me." Endz was as dumbfounded as Dana and he let her get comfortable in his arms.

Momma Flo, Miles, and Dominique observed Endz and Dana's interaction throughout the birthday party and right now at this very moment. No words were exchanged but they all had the same idea. Endz queen was resting in his arms.

As the movie played, Dana's phone rang. "Oh, I'm sorry. I forgot to put this thing on silent." Dana looked at her phone, saw it was Neil calling again, and pressed ignore. She turned off her phone completely and put her phone back. "There we go," she said and went back to enjoying the movie all snuggled in Endz's arms.

Girl quit bullshitting and get with a real nigga that's right there in your face! Dominique wanted to say to her best friend on the outside, but ended up screaming it on the inside.

*****

"Dana pick up your motherfucking phone right now!" Neil screamed in his phone on Dana's voicemail. He looked over at Patresha who was sitting on her bed in her room in tears. They had the place to themselves because Lexus had a date with Wyatt, she was spending the night at his apartment.

Patresha really wanted to go with Dominique to Momma Flo's birthday party, but Neil called and wanted to come over. He begged and sweet-talked her into cancelling her plans and giving Dominique an excuse to cover it up. She reluctantly agreed thinking that he would apologize for the other night. Most of the evening all he did was blow up Dana's phone as if

Patresha wasn't even in the room and it was fucking with her. Not to mention, he was checking out Instagram models while sitting right next to her. He had her slave over a hot stove cooking his dinner and washing the dishes while he did him and paid her no attention.

"What the fuck is your problem?" Neil asked with annoyance at Patresha's tears.

"You keep calling her and not paying any atten..."

Whap!

Neil cut off Patresha's crying and whining by slapping her hard across the face. "It ain't your motherfucking business who the fuck I'm calling! You should be lucky I'm giving your ass another chance after that shit you pulled at the club!"

"Lexus and Be-vo were only looking out for me after you stood me up and..."

"Shut the fuck up!" Neil crudely interrupted. "Shut your whining fat ass up!" He yanked his pants down and ordered, "Suck this dick, bitch!"

Patresha got on her knees and put Neil's seven-inch dick in her mouth. She sucked it hard so he could hurry up and nut. Neil looked down at Patresha and got turned on by the power he had over the low self-esteem having college freshman. He felt like the man having a side chick that was totally under his control. He didn't think Patresha was suitable enough for him to have on his arm in public. She was just fine in the bedroom.

Darnella and his other side hoes he had no problem flaunting around in public, but Dana was the love of his life. He just had to slap her around once in a while to keep her in line. Her leaving him was fucking with him. He didn't know where the fuck she was. She could be laid up with some other nigga for all he knew. If he were to ever find out that she's giving his pussy away to another nigga, there would be hell to pay.

Patresha had excellent dick sucking skills. Neil didn't wanna cum in her mouth. "That's enough!" Neil pulled Patresha by her hair away from his groin. "Now get undressed and lay on your *Pillsbury Doughboy* stomach!"

Into the Arms of His Boss

Patresha got on her feet and did exactly as she was told. She slowly got undressed and Neil slipped out of his pants and boxers. Patresha laid on her stomach on her bed and Neil jumped on top of her. He roughly shoved all his dick up Patresha's ass without any warming.

"Ouch, it hurts!" Patresha screamed with extreme pain. Neil began to pound Patresha's asshole with great force.

"Please! Stop! It hurts!" Patresha couldn't take the pain. "Please stop!" Her cries were falling on Neil's deaf ears as he used his dick to rip apart Patresha's anus. The more she begged and cried the harder Neil fucked her ass. Her crying and begging meant nothing to Neil. In fact, the more Patresha beg and cried the more sexually exited the sick fuck got. In his mind, Patresha had better been grateful that any man wanted to have any type of sex with her. Pleasurable or not.

Patresha thought the anal torture would never end until she felt Neil's big load of cum shooting into her asshole. Neil collapsed on top of her as he nutted deep inside her. Patresha was glad it was over. Neil climbed off of her and found his pants and boxers to put back on.

"Shit that was great!" Neil felt like a new man. "And I forgive you for embarrassing me at the club."

Patresha didn't say anything. She was in a trance from shame and humiliation with her asshole busted wide opened. She could even feel it starting to bleed mixed with Neil's cum. She was paralyzed in shock with her eyes wide opened and tears running down her cheeks.

Neil laughed on the inside, but he knew he had to take a different approach in order to keep Patresha's mouth shut. He laid in bed next to her and wrapped his arms around her. "Patresha, I'm sorry I was a little rough. You know I didn't mean for it to hurt."

"You hit me, called me fat, and hurt me," Patresha found her voice and wiped her tears. "I told you it hurt, but you didn't listen to me."

"I was caught up in the moment. You know how much I

71

enjoy making love to you, baby. I'm sorry I hit you and for being mean to you. I was just upset and hurt about what you pulled at the club." Neil was playing his mind games, acting like he was the victim. "I understand you felt like you was stood up, but something came up."

"With that woman, you were hugging all over?" Patresha referred to Darnella who pushed her and was making fun of her.

"She's just an old friend," Neil continued to lie through his motherfucking teeth. "She said she really wanted to see me, and I lost track of the time. The reason I blew you off was because she's the jealous type and I didn't want to do anything to drive her crazy."

"What about Ms. Dana? You're still chasing after her. Even after she left you to be with her real baby daddy. Why is she still wearing your engagement ring?" Patresha noted that detail when she had to work under Dana during her internship.

Neil was getting pissed off with all these fucking questions, but he had to maintain his composure in order to calm Patresha down, so she wouldn't do anything stupid like run her mouth to anybody about him. "That's just until the baby is born, and we get the DNA test to see if the baby is mine."

Patresha was still in doubt and Neil knew he had to dig deeper. "Patresha, I love you with all my heart and I want us to be together. I promise that I will never hurt you again. You just have to be patient with me. You believe in me, don't you?"

Patresha was still not sure about Neil. "Well..."

"Please believe in me," Neil's begging could put Keith Sweat to shame. His ass would've made a great actor with four or five Academy Awards under his belt. "It would really hurt me if you stopped believing in me." He managed to let a single tear fall from his eye. He was really doing the most.

That tear did it for Patresha. All of her doubts and concerns disappeared with that tear. "Yes, Neil. I believe in you!"

"That's my girl! I love you!" Neil kissed Patresha.

"I love you too!" Patresha said and they cuddled and started to make out. Neil climbed on top of her and gently slid his dick inside her pussy.

What a dumb fat bitch! Neil thought as he gave Patresha her first orgasm for the night.

Jamila

Chapter 12
2002

"Dana, do you have your last bag packed?" Veronica asked a six-year-old Dana.

"Yes momma," Dana answered while holding her pink and purple suitcase with cute little teddy bears all over it.

"Good girl!" Veronica hugged her little girl. "Eli and Nicky are on their way with the car and we're gonna move in with Nicky's grandma."

"Momma Flo is very nice! I can't wait!" Dana was excited. She always felt loved and safe in the presence of Momma Flo. Being inside her home was like a fairyland to her.

After sixteen years of marriage, Veronica reached her breaking point. She had enough of her so-called husband, Lando's abuse. After another ass beating, Lando walked out and hasn't been seen or heard from in over a week. Veronica guessed he was probably laid up with one of his many whores.

Veronica used this golden opportunity to pack her and her children's things and move out before Lando came back. Most of their things were already packed up and in storage. Now they just have a few bags to put in the car to retreat to their safe haven which was Momma Flo's house. Only this time it'll be home until Veronica got back on her feet.

Veronica and Dana grabbed the bags, walked downstairs and into the living room. They patiently sat on the couch waiting for Eli and Endz to come back with the car they borrowed from the drug dealer they work under. Of course, Veronica didn't like Eli's choice of income because of the dangers that come with it. Eli assured her that he'd be fine. He was saving enough money for their escape and he'll go legit when the time is right. Veronica was a little relieved with Endz by her baby's side. He's loyal and both book and street smart. In fact, he's been offered scholarships to multiple colleges and on his way to be class valedictorian. Until the time is right, they gotta do what they gotta do.

"*Where are they?*" *Veronica was anxious with Dana in her arms. Dana didn't want her momma to worry. She didn't know what to say to calm her mother's nerves. All she could do was kiss her on the cheek. Veronica loved Dana's kisses. The door opened and when Veronica saw who was entering the house she was in complete shock.*

"*I'm back!*" *Lando announced himself like everything was all good after beating his wife and disappearing. He saw his wife and daughter sitting on the couch speechless. They had nothing to say to him.*

Lando looked over at Veronica and yelled, "*What the fuck is your problem? Something wrong with your fucking hearing?*" *Veronica not saying a word was pissing him off. He looked down and saw packed bags on the floor.* "*What the fuck is this shit?*"

Veronica knew there would be hell to pay when she gave her answer, but at this point, she's been living in hell for sixteen years and today was gonna be her last day in it whether she lives through it or not.

"*There's no easy way to say this.*" *Veronica sighed.* "*I'm leaving you. I can't take it anymore.*"

"*You can't take what?*" *Lando's blood was boiling.*

"*I wasted my life with you!*" *Veronica got off the couch nice and easy, standing tall to make her point more crystal clear.* "*I'm leaving you!*" *she repeated.* "*It's over! I'm done! I'm done with your beatings, disrespect, and*

cheating! I've had enough! It's time for us to..."

Whap!

Lando leaped over and pimp slapped Veronica, making her fall hard on the floor. "*You fucking ungrateful bitch!*" *he yelled and jumped on top of her.*

"*Stop please!*" *Veronica pleaded and Lando answered with a punch to the face.*

"*Stop what?*"

Punch!

You think you just gonna leave me! Who is he?"

"*What are you talking about?*" *Veronica tried to break free, but he had her pinned down.*

"Who the fuck is he?" Lando pulled Veronica by her hair and screamed in her face. "Answer me bitch!"

"I knew your filthy hoe ass was fucking around on me! Well you ain't getting away with it, bitch!" He yanked Veronica off the floor by her hair.

"Daddy stop hurting mommy!" Little Dana begged with tears in her eyes.

Lando ignored his daughter's cries and threw Veronica on the couch and growled. "Since your ass wanna be a hoe! That's what the fuck you about to be treated like!"

Lando was in the process of unbuckling his pants when he was getting pulled back by Eli and Endz. "Let go!" He struggled.

"You ain't gonna hurt my momma again! Bitch ass mother-fucker!" Eli punched his father in the face.

Over the years, Eli lost a lot of respect for Lando as a father and as a man. He got in excellent shape so he could be able to defend his mother and baby sister. Endz joined his best friend and they both started tearing Lando's ass up. Eli looked down at his pathetic excuse of a sperm donor who beats his wife but can't fight off two teenage boys.

"Endz get the rope. It's in the trunk," Eli instructed.

"I got it." Endz nodded his head and walked out the door.

Eli walked over to Veronica and Dana, asking them, "Are y'all alright?"

"Yes, Eli." Dana gave her big brother a hug.

"I will be," Veronica struggled to answer with a swollen lip.

Lando looked at his younger carbon copy comforting Veronica and Dana and was disgusted. He thought it was pathetic and pussified watching his son playing Captain Save A Hoe to his mother. "You worthless, little, pussy, punk bit..."

Endz shut Lando up with a powerful right hook and knocked his ass out cold. He tied Lando's hands behind his back and tied his wrists up with the rope.

"Come here, Dana." Eli lifted his beautiful baby sister off

the ground and carried her out of the house while Endz helped Veronica clean up her bruises before getting the bags.

Eli carried Dana and headed to the black Ford Expedition. He opened the back door, placed Dana inside, and fastened her seatbelt. "There you go, baby girl! It's gonna be okay!"

"I was scared Eli," Dana said with a little sniffle.

"You ain't gotta be scared anymore, baby girl." Eli used his thumb to wipe Dana's tears away. "You always got me and Endz to protect you. We'll make sure nothing happens to you and momma, okay?"

"Okay."

"Now, you stay here while I go check on momma and help Endz out, but before I go." Eli reached in the front passenger seat and grabbed a pink gift bag. He reached into the bag to reveal a stuffed pink dinosaur and gave it to Dana. "Here you go! I got this for you!"

"Yay! Thanks, Eli!" Dana cheered and hugged her new stuffed toy night and tight. "I love you!" She jumped into Eli's arms and kissed his cheek.

"I love you too, baby girl!"

*****

"What's up, Dana?" Endz interrupted her daze. She was lying in the bed with her bathrobe on after a nice and relaxing bubble bath. She was holding her stuffed pink dinosaur thinking about her big brother, Eli, and how he protected her and their mother.

"Hey Endz. What's up?" Dana sat up in the bed.

"I have some documents I need you to look over for me." Endz handed Dana his tablet so she can look over the documents he downloaded.

"Sure thing."

Endz saw Dana put aside her stuffed pink dinosaur. "You still have that stuffed pink dinosaur?"

"Yes, I do! In fact, I was thinking back to the day Eli gave me this. I will never part with this thing. I can't thank you and Momma Flo enough for helping us out." Dana held Endz hand.

"No problem." Endz kissed Dana's hand. "You know that's what grandma do, and I was helping my boy out."

"And y'all did a great job."

"Listen. I gotta get ready for my appointment. You just give me back the tablet when you're done."

"Okay."

Endz got off the bed and left the room. Dana looked through the documents thoroughly and made mental notes for her report. Dana loved her career and being a businesswoman. She was also excited about becoming a mother. Now if only her future husband can just act right.

"All done!" Dana exclaimed after reviewing the last document.

Dana grabbed the tablet and headed to the master bedroom where Endz laid his head. She opened the door without a second thought. "Endz, here's the..." She froze when she saw Endz standing a few feet away from her... naked.

"Oh, uh...huh..."

"You good, Dana?" Endz asked calmly without any shame.

"Yeah...it's just..." Dana couldn't help but notice Endz's sexy ass body. From the tattoos on his chest and right arm all the way down to his rock hard, thick, nine-inch dick. This was Dana's first time seeing a dick that didn't belong to Neil live and in person. In fact, this was the second dick she'd ever seen in person in her whole life. Her pussy started to get moist and tingle from the sight of that dick.

Oh, shit it even has a hook in it! Dana couldn't believe she was lusting over another man's dick. Not just any man's dick; this was the dick of her childhood friend. Her brother's best friend. He's also her and her fiancé's employer. Sure, Neil got a dick, but Endz got dick, dick! She shook her head to get those types of nasty, yet sexy, thoughts out of her head. She didn't forget she was a respectable engaged woman who is carrying the man she was supposed to marry baby. But one last look wouldn't hurt.

After her final look, Dana said, "Here's your tablet....and can you cover up please?"

"You know it's situations like this is the reason why people usually knock first before they enter a room." Endz grabbed the tablet.

"My bad." She blushed with embarrassment.

"No, you good." Endz grabbed his bathrobe and put it on. "Nice to know that I'm still sexy as fuck."

Dana was taken aback. "Excuse you?"

"Well, you didn't exactly cover your eyes or run for the door. And you staring at my dick doesn't really help your case much either."

"Okay, you got me," Dana confessed and laughed it off. "I liked what I saw. I'll let you get to your appointment." She turned around to leave but not before adding, "By the way, your future lady is a very lucky woman." *What the fuck did I just say?* Dana has never been that bold before.

"Why thank you." Endz chuckled a little bit and blushed.

Ring! Ring!

The doorbell rang. "Come on."

"Alright," Dana said and let Endz grab her hand and led her out of his bedroom.

Dana didn't know what was going on, but she trusted Endz completely. They went down the stairs and towards the front door. Endz answered the door and there stood two beautiful women who were identical twin sisters dressed in all white with two massage tables. "Hello Mr. Washington," they greeted.

"Hello, Helga. Hello Chay. Come in," Endz greeted and let the ladies in the house and closed the door. Despite the ladies being identical twin sisters, it was easy to tell them apart. Chay was fifty pounds heavier than Helga. "This is my childhood friend and business partner, Dana Spicer," he introduced.

"Hello, ladies." Dana smiled and the ladies greeted back. There was something Endz said that kind of left Dana puzzled and wanted to address it. "Business partner? Is that what you call

all of your employees, Mr. Washington?"

"Only the ones closest to me who I one hundred percent trust." Endz winked at Dana.

"I'm flattered." Endz was making Dana feel so special and important. Neil needed to take lessons from Endz on how to treat women. Dana then saw two massage tables set up for Endz massage appointment. "You need two tables for a massage, Endz? Is life that stressful my nigga?"

"One of them is for you," Endz said.

"Are you serious?"

"Yep. Chay will take great care of you."

"Right this way, Ms. Spicer," Chay directed Dana to her specially designed massage table for pregnant women.

"Thank you." Dana was about to take off her robe, but something stopped her. She glanced over at Endz awkwardly who was getting a rub down from Helga.

Endz saw the look on Dana's face. "Why you acting all shy for? You already saw my naked ass."

Dana went ahead and dropped her robe to the floor and let Chay help her on the table. "Happy now? We're even," Dana said to Endz.

"Very happy," Endz said and admired Dana's sexy body. Her succulent double D titties. That plentiful ass and thick thighs. Her baby bump made her look even sexier. A woman carrying another human being in her body takes a lot of strength and sacrifice. That's what made Dana beautiful and sexy in Endz eyes.

Chay's hands felt so good on Dana's skin. She did a great job using her hands to relieve all the tension from her body. Dana really needed this.

"Ooooh, this feels so good!" Dana moaned out. "Thank you for this Endz." Dana grabbed Endz hand as she was enjoying the massage.

"Anytime, baby girl," Endz said and kissed her hand. "You deserve the best."

Which is right in front of you, Helga and Chay shared the

same thought from witnessing the interaction.

Chapter 13

"Where the fuck is she at?" Neil impatiently waited for Dana at The Flint restaurant.

It took some time for Dana to agree to the meeting. Dana was gonna say no, but she knew Neil wouldn't back off until she agreed to meet him. Plus, she needed to limit her stress during her pregnancy. She hoped after this meeting Neil will understand and give her the space that she needs so she can think about her life, Neil, and their baby.

"Bitch, where the fuck are you?" Neil wanted Dana back now. Not now, but right motherfucking now. Not knowing where Dana was living these days was fucking with him.

Neil couldn't stand all this waiting. He had a good mind to drag Dana and lay into her ass as soon as she walked through the door. Neil looked up and saw Dana walk through the door. She looked absolutely stunning. She looked around the restaurant to find Neil. When she found him, she made her way towards his table.

As she was walking, several men that she passed by was checking her out which angered Neil. Dana knew this and was slightly flattered by the attention which pissed off Neil even further.

The second Dana was at the table, Neil didn't waste any time unleashing his anger towards her. "Glad your ass finally showed up. I told your ass to be here at six!"

Not this shit! Dana rolled her eyes and took a seat across from Neil. "Nigga calm your ass down. First of all, it is six o'clock." Neil looked at his phone and saw that it was six o'clock on the dot. "Also, be grateful that I even came at all. In fact, I didn't even wanna be here in the first place, but it was the only way to get you to stop blowing up my phone. And since I'm in a good mood today, I'll excuse the fact that you lacked the basic common decency to properly greet me."

Who the fuck does she think she is talking to like that? Neil thought. He was losing control over Dana and he hated it. That's why he needed her back so he can control her again.

"So, what's up?" Dana wanted to get this over with so she can go.

"Come home!" Neil ordered.

"That was it?" Dana asked. "That was the reason you wanted to meet with me. Not asking about this baby or how I'm doing or changing your abusive, cheating and disrespectful ways?"

"I told you that I was sorry about that shit!"

"I'm gonna need a little bit more time," Dana said. "You brought that hoe into our home, you disrespected me and tried to drown me."

"Come on baby. I'm sorry," Neil tried to sweet-talk his way out of it. "You know I love you, baby. I was just playing."

Dana couldn't help but laugh at this shit because it was funny as fuck. "Really! You were just playing? Boy, you so crazy!"

Dana kept on laughing and Neil joined in. "Yeah, that's right. I was just playing. You understand, don't you baby?" Neil was confident that he won Dana over.

"Yeah, so you were just playing when you said I sucked in bed to justify fucking Darnella, pushed me in the pool and tried to drown me, and then ran off to take her back to her house to fuck until the sun came up."

Dana's laughter continued. She then started to laugh harder and crazier. The crazy laugh caught the attention of everybody in the restaurant. By this time, Neil stopped laughing and found the whole thing a little embarrassing.

After a few more minutes, Dana immediately stopped laughing and looked at Neil with scorn and disgust. "Nigga please! I'm out!"

Dana got out of her seat and headed for the door. She thought this meeting would be a waste of time, but humiliating Neil made the trip worth it. Neil opened the door with that dumb ass bullshit explanation and Dana jumped on the opportunity.

Neil dashed after her out of the restaurant and into the parking lot. "Dana! Come back!" He caught up with her and grabbed her arm. "Where the fuck you going?"

Dana snatched her arm away and yelled. "None of your motherfucking business!"

"We ain't finished talking!"

"Oh yes, the fuck we are!"

Neil squeezed Dana's face hard and hissed in her face. "Oh no, the fuck we're not!"

Dana pushed Neil away. Neil balled up his fist and raises it up ready to punch Dana. "I wouldn't do that if I were you." Dana motioned her head to her right. There was a police car with a cop inside and across the street was a group of people walking towards the restaurant. Neil slowly put his fist down.

"Neil, you have a problem," Dana said. "Listen, I love you. I want to marry you and start a beautiful family with you, but what I'm not gonna do is be your punching bag. If you want me back, you gotta earn me back. You want me to come back home? Do you really love me and our baby? Prove it!" On that note, Dana turned around to take her leave.

"How the fuck am I supposed to do that?" Neil yelled.

"Motherfucker figure it out!" Dana yelled out her answer as she kept on walking.

Neil was so frustrated. He pulled out his phone to make a call. "Hey, baby!"

"Hey, Darnella! How you doing, baby girl," Neil greeted with a smile.

"I'm good! How are you?"

"Dana pissed me off again." Nail put on his victim hat.

"I don't know why you let that bitch stress you. She ain't worth it." Darnella sympathized.

"You are so good to me. You wanna come over to my house?" Neil needed a good fuck and he knew he could get that from Darnella.

"I'm sorry, baby. I'm not in town. I'm in New York."

"Awe. When you coming back?"

"In about four days."

"I'll be waiting for you or I can come up there if you want,"

Neil suggested. He could use a vacation.

"Alright! Just let me know when you're on your way. I can't wait to see you," Darnella said. "Bye baby."

"Bye." Neil ended the call.

Neil couldn't wait to see Darnella to get some of that good pussy and head. If only Dana would let Darnella teach her how to fuck, but oh well. He still needed to get his dick wet. He searched through his contacts and found the number he saved as Fat Hoe. He dialed the number. It rang twice and it went to voicemail.

"Did this fat bitch just ignore me?" Neil called Patresha again and still the same thing. Ring twice and then voicemail. "Yes, her fat ass did ignore me!" Then he sent a text.

Neil: *Pick up the fucking phone!*

"That bitch don't know who the fuck I am!" Neil got a reply and looked at the message.

Patresha: *I can't talk right now. I'm studying.*
Neil: *I don't give a fuck! I want some pussy! NOW!*
Patresha: *I can't. I got shit to do. Go ask Ms. Dana or your hoe from the club!*

Neil couldn't believe this shit! It's bad enough that Dana walked out on him and Darnella was out of town, but he'd be damned if he was gonna be tossed to the side by the likes of Patresha Glover.

Neil: *Who the fuck do you think you talking to?*
Patresha: *I'm sick of your disrespectful shit!*
Neil: *I don't have time to listen to your whining fat ass. You better pick up this damn phone.*
Patresha: *And I told you that I was studying. Now if you start being nicer to me, then maybe I'll think about meeting up with you later but until then goodbye.*

Into the Arms of His Boss

Neil was seething like a motherfucker! How dare Patresha disrespect him like that. "Oh, that bitch wanna play? Then let's motherfucking play!"

Jamila

Chapter 14

"This is beautiful!" Dominique smiled and kissed her husband in the bedroom of their cabin in Blue Ridge, Georgia. They were looking out the window admiring the beautiful mountains.

"Yes, it is." Miles had his arms wrapped around Dominique.

"This getaway was a great idea," Dominique said.

"Yes, it was. This has been the best three days ever."

Dominique turned around to face Miles. "I have an idea."

"Oh really?" Miles kissed Dominique.

Dominique didn't say anything. She giggled and took Miles by the hand. She presented the chair for him to take a seat. She pulled out her phone to play the song "Naked" by Adina Howard and put it on repeat. She strutted over to Miles and began to give him a lap dance. Miles loved his wife's sexy curves as they matched the beat to the song.

Dominique slowly unbuttoned her white shirt and opened it to expose her candy apple red bra covering her double D titties. As she bent over, she took off her black jeans to reveal her red and black, polka-dot thong exposing her ass. Miles leaned over to grab a handful of that big juicy ass. Dominique was Miles' favorite stripper. Not just because she's his wife. It's because of her beauty, skills and he can actually touch her and fuck her.

Dominique turned around and giggled. She loved the way Miles grabbed her ass. She moved her body to the music as she took off her bra to let her big and beautiful tits free. She sat on Miles' lap and took her right titty and put it in his mouth for him to suck. His tongue felt so good all over her nipple. Dominique put her hand between her legs and started rubbing her clit through her thong. She let out a soft moan.

Dominique felt Miles' dick getting hard through his pants. She got up from his lap and got on both knees in front of him.

Dominique was about to take off his pants to suck his dick, but he stopped her. "No! I want that pussy!" Miles got out of the chair and lifted Dominique off the floor. He placed her on the bed and took off his clothes. The sight of his muscular body and thick fat dick with his big ass balls hanging low made Dominique take off her thong with the quickness and throw it across the room. Miles pressed his weight on top of her and slid his dick deep inside her sweet wet pussy.

Feeling her juices all over his dick and the tightness of her pussy drove him crazy. He held Dominique close to him as he dug deeper in her pussy. She screamed with pleasure as she tightened her pussy muscles on his dick. She wanted all that dick deep inside her. This was some bomb ass dick and it was all hers. She loved nutting all over it and making it wet with her sweet tasty pussy juices.

"Oh shit!" Dominique moaned as she came for the infinite time. "Oh, baby!" Dominique held onto Miles tight as she busted another nut.

"Ooooh fuck!" Miles stroked harder to make Dominique cum again. "Oh shit, girl! This pussy is so good!"

"Mmmm! Yes, baby! This is your pussy, baby!" Dominique screamed with pleasure and kissed Miles.

"This right!" Miles moaned. "Say that shit again!"

"This your pussy, daddy!"

"Louder!"

"This your pussy, daddy!"

Their lovemaking was very intense. Miles picked up the pace when he felt like he was about to cum. He made sure to dump his load deep inside that pussy.

Dominique and Miles cuddled in each other's arms in their beautiful afterglow. "Mmmm! I can't get enough of this dick," Dominique purred and rubbed Miles' dick.

"Is that right?" Miles smiled with confidence. He knew he put it down, but it's nice to hear his woman say it.

"Yep." They kissed.

"And I love tearing this pussy up." Miles gave Dominique's cum covered clit a quick rub and grabbed her ass with both hands. "So tight, wet, and juicy."

"Mmmm! Let's hope we finally have positive pregnancy test results," Dominique said.

"We will baby," Miles said.

"I mean we've been trying for years and no luck," Dominique said with doubt. Dominique and Miles' biggest dream was to have children and start a family. They didn't realize it would be harder than they thought.

"It'll happen for us baby," Miles assured and held Dominique said. "When the time comes, we'll welcome our beautiful little bundle of joy. He'll have my looks and your ride or die loyalty."

"Or she'll look just like her mommy with her daddy's boss presence," Dominique added another scenario.

"Right! Right!"

"Imagine. Our babies." The thought of being parents brought joy to Dominique's heart. "They'll be friends with Dana's baby. I know Patresha will be a wonderful aunty."

"And Endz, momma, Oliver, and grandma love the kids," Miles said. "Whether it's a boy or a girl, I know one thing for sure."

"What's that baby?"

"They'll have a wonderful mother and father in their lives."

"That's right," Dominique agreed and laid her head on Miles' chest.

After a few moments of rest, Miles' dick got hard again. "Let me slide in them guts again."

"I'm game!" He didn't have to tell Dominique twice. She opened her legs and let Miles climb on top of her to make love again.

This was the life. A beautiful love story that started in the club. Miles asked Dominique to dance and they danced until the club was ready to close. He was so into the beauty that he forgot to ask for her name and phone number as she walked out the door. From that night, all he could think about was the beauty in the lime green dress. Miles thought he would never see her again until he was in a board meeting when Endz introduced the new colleagues of the company and there she was.

He had to get at her and make her his so after the meeting he properly introduced himself and the rest is history. Having the perfect life as husband and wife. All that's missing is children which they hope will change soon.

Deep into their lovemaking session, Dominique's phone rings. "Let's just ignore that," Dominique moaned out and Miles didn't argue with her. Then the phone rang again. Dominique figured whoever it was they were not gonna stop calling until they get an answer. She gently pushed Miles off of her and climbed out of bed.

"Hey, where are you going?' Miles pouted.

"Nigga, I'm coming back!" Dominique chuckled at Miles acting like a big spoiled baby and found her phone.

"It's Lexus," Dominique said to Miles before taking the call. "Hey, Lexus. What's up? Lexus, I can't understand what you're saying. You gotta calm down," Dominique's eyes widened with fear when she heard Lexus talk and it concerned Miles. "What! What the fuck! Shit, I'll be right there!" She hung up.

"Dominique, what's wrong?" Miles hopped out of bed to console her.

"Patresha is in the hospital!" Dominique was in a panic frantically putting on her clothes and packing all her shit.

"Fuck!" Miles started putting on his clothes.

"We gotta go back to Albany right motherfucking now! Shit, let her be okay! I love that girl!" Dominique was nervously shaken up.

"She will be." Miles tried to calm Dominique down. "Let's get going."

"Okay," Dominique took a deep breath to try to calm down. "Thanks for understanding."

"Understanding about what?"

"Cutting our trip short."

"Baby fuck all of that. Patresha is family and I love her. Family over everything!"

Before leaving the cabin, Dominique said to Miles, "Thank you for being a good man to me."

"Anytime," Miles responded with a quick kiss before they

headed back to Albany.

Jamila

Chapter 15

"Look at there! Look at our baby girl!" Dana glowed with joy at the sonogram with Neil sitting by her side as they enjoyed their lunch at a Jamaican restaurant.

"Amazing!" Neil smiled. "It was nice sharing this moment with you." He grabbed Dana's hand and kissed it. "Thanks, baby. Again, I'm sorry for my behavior. You deserve better and I promise to try to be that for you."

"Those words are beautiful, but actions speak a lot louder," Dana said.

"I understand." Neil nodded. "You enjoying your food?"

"Yes, and thanks for taking me out to lunch."

"Of course! I gotta feed my baby." Neil kissed Dana. Since everything was peaceful between them, she allowed the kiss. "Both of my babies." Neil rubbed Dana's pregnant belly and kissed it.

"Bae, you so silly!" Dana laughed.

"Mmmm! That smile. I miss that beautiful and sexy smile," Neil said.

"Thank you," Dana said. "And I miss this charming man. See you can be sweet when you wanna be."

"Neil?" A beautiful young woman with caramel skin with dark brown eyes approached their table. "Neil, it's great to see you."

"Hi Sarina," Neil greeted. "Dana, this is Dr. Sarina Smith. Sarina this is Dana, my fiancée."

"Oh yes, Dana. Neil's told me so much about you during our sessions," Sarina said.

"He has?" Dana was pleasantly surprised that Neil was going to therapy. She wondered why Neil didn't mention it before. Oh well as long as he was getting help was all that mattered to Dana.

"Yes, he's told me about how he can't wait to marry you and be a father," Sarina volunteered.

"Oooh, y'all are making me blush. Would you like to sit down and join us?" Dana invited Sarina.

"Oh, I don't wanna intrude," Sarina politely declined.

"Oh, it's no trouble at all," Dana insisted. "I would like to get to know the person who is helping my fiancé."

"Well okay." Sarina accepted the invitation and took a seat.

"Neil, when did you start going to therapy?" Dana asked.

"I thought about what you said at The Flint and it really opened my eyes." Neil grabbed Dana's hand and rubbed it with care while looking deep into her eyes. "I realized I needed help, but I didn't know where to start. Then I heard about Sarina and gave her a call."

Dana turned to Sarina and asked, "How's he doing?"

"He's a work in progress, but then again everybody that comes through my door is a work in progress," Sarina answered. "As long as they're willing to take that first step and do the work, anything is possible."

"Exactly!" Dana agreed. Her phone began to ring. "Excuse me." She dug in her purse to grab her phone. She saw it was Dominique calling and answered. "Hey, girl! What's up? How's the vacation?"

"Dana, we're back in Albany. We're at the hospital!" Dominique was in complete distress.

"You're at the hospital? Why?" Dana asked with concern as Neil and Sarina quietly listened.

"It's Patresha! Somebody rammed into her car, pulled her out of the car, and started beating her!" Dominique was hysterical.

"Oh my God! Are you serious?" Dana couldn't believe what Dominique just told her. Who would do something like that to a completely innocent girl?

"Hell yeah! Lexus called and told me!"

"What's Patresha's condition right now?"

"She's still unconscious, but the doctors said she should make a full recovery."

"Alright, I'll be right there." Dana hung up and got out of her seat to be by her best friend's side.

"What's wrong, baby?" Neil asked.

96

"Dominique's little sister was attacked."

"I'm sorry to hear that," Sarina offered her sympathy.

"I gotta go to the hospital," Dana said still in a daze.

"I'll come with you," Neil offered and got out of his seat to console Dana.

"Thanks." Dana turned to Sarina and said, "I'm sorry for rushing off like this. It was nice meeting you."

"I understand. It was nice meeting you too and I hope everything turns out okay," Sarina said.

"Me too."

Jamila

Chapter 16

"How is she, doctor? Any updates?" Dominique frantically asked the doctor with Miles' arms around her in one of the waiting rooms of Phoebe Putney Memorial Hospital.

"There are no broken bones, but she's still unconscious. We're trying to bring her out of it now," the doctor reported.

"Thank you, Doctor," Dominique said with relief and the doctor went on his way.

"I can't wait to get my hands on the bastard or bitch that did this!" Dominique seethed with anger.

"Don't worry baby." Miles held her tighter. "They're gonna get theirs."

"We're back," Wyatt announced with Lexus on his arm as they approached Dominique and Miles.

"How is she?" Lexus was anxious to know the current condition of her honorary sister.

"She's still unconscious, but no serious life-threatening injuries. The doctors are trying to wake her up now." Miles repeated the doctor's report.

"Thank God!" Lexus sighed with relief.

"What's up? Is Patresha okay?" Be-vo appeared out of nowhere and asked.

"She's still unconscious, but she should make a full recovery. No serious damage," Wyatt told him.

"We appreciate you coming by Bellamy," Dominique said with gratitude.

"You know you can just call me Be-vo."

"Yeah, but you're not DJing right now, so it's Bellamy," Dominique flashed a fake ass smile while patting Be-vo on the top of his head and almost messing up his freshly done cornrows. She always thought Be-vo was a dumb name. She knew it was his stage name, but still. She liked Bellamy better.

Dominique then saw Dana and Neil walking towards them. "Oh look! Dana's here!" She rushed over to Dana and gave her a hug. "Hey girl!"

"How you holding up? How's Patresha?" Dana asked.

"She'll be okay, but still unconscious. Me, on the other hand, I'm all over the motherfucking place. Hi, Neil," Dominique politely greeted.

"Hello!" Neil greeted back.

Miles excused himself to use the bathroom and left Lexus, Wyatt, and Be-vo alone. Be-vo looked over at the couple Dominique was talking to and quickly recognized Neil. "Wait a minute. Isn't that the nigga I had to fuck up at the club?"

Wyatt and Lexus gave each other a crazy look like they knew something Be-vo didn't, which was completely true. Lexus told Wyatt everything that went down at the club when he got back from his trip. "Uh...Uh..." The two stuttered.

"Yes, the fuck it is!" Be-vo concluded.

"Oh shit!" Wyatt shrieked and he and Lexus pulled Be-vo away.

"What the fuck!" Be-vo struggled as Lexus and Wyatt pulled him into a vacant waiting room. When they were sure that nobody could hear them, they let Be-vo go.

Be-vo took a moment to collect himself. "Alright. Now that I'm all cool, calm, and collected." He turned to Wyatt and called him, "Nigga," while still maintaining his cool he turned to Lexus and called her, "Niggette, will you two motherfuckers be so kind and explain to me what the fuck is going on?" He requested in a way that you would talk to a two-year-old child.

"It's a very long story, Be-vo," Lexus answered with a nervous smile.

"I have all the time in the motherfucking world." Be-vo was not backing down. He wanted an explanation and he wanted one right motherfucking now. "So that fuck nigga got a whole woman and I saw that fat ass rock on her left finger."

"Yes," Wyatt confessed. He figured he and Lexus might as well fill in the blanks.

"While he is seeing my girl, Patresha?" Be-vo was keeping his anger under control. It wasn't easy, but he managed to do so.

"Yes," Lexus answered.

100

"Hold on a second." Be-vo began to walk out of the waiting room. Wyatt was about to stop him, but Be-vo assured him, "I ain't going nowhere." Be-vo peeked around the corner to take a good look at Dana. He thought she was a beautiful and sweet looking woman. *How did a complete fuckboy scoop her up?* As he was studying Dana's appearance, he zeroed in on her midsection. He was in more shock than he already was. He then went back into the waiting room to join Wyatt and Lexus. "She has a bun in the oven too?"

"Yes," Wyatt and Lexus answered.

"Alright somebody better tell me something! What the fuck is going on?"

Lexus sighed before letting Be-vo in on everything. "Patresha and I have been interning for Mr. Washington's company. Ms. Dana is a childhood friend of his and she works for him and sometimes we work under her. She's engaged to Neil and pregnant with his baby."

"Okay, I got all of that. Now explain how Patresha got mixed up with that bastard," Be-vo pressed for more.

Lexus went on with the story. "We met them at Mr. Washington's party at his house. Dominique and Miles took us as a learning experience. Miles is Mr. Washington's little cousin and Dominique and Ms. Dana are best friends."

"So, this nigga is so low down he'll fuck around on his pregnant fiancée with her best friend's baby sister." Be-vo put his arms around Wyatt and Lexus. "Thank y'all for pulling me away because I was gonna give him another ass whopping."

"Well, I think Patresha is over him for good," Lexus said.

"Let's hope so," Be-vo said. "Go on," He instructed Lexus to finish the fucked-up story.

"During the party, Patresha and Neil ran into each other. They talked for a little bit and he sweet-talked his way into getting her number and the rest has been a complete fucking nightmare," Lexus finished.

"Ms. Dana seems like a sweet woman. She deserves better," Be-vo said.

"We can only hope she does find better," Wyatt said.

"Let's get back and check on Patresha," Be-vo said and started to walk out of the waiting room.

"Wait a minute." Wyatt stopped Be-vo. "Can you handle being around Neil?"

"No, but I can fake it," Be-vo answered honestly. "Besides, I don't think he's stupid enough to try anything with his fiancée around."

"Good point." Lexus nodded in agreement and the three made their way back to Patresha's hospital room.

"Oh, y'all made it back just in time," Miles said when he saw the three young adults approaching.

"She's awake," Dominique said with joy.

"That's great!" Lexus cheered. "We'll let y'all go in first." She pointed at Dominique and Miles.

"Okay!" Dominique hugged Lexus and she and Miles entered Patresha's room. "Hey, baby girl!" Dominique rushed over to her baby sister's bedside and hugged her.

"Dominique!" Patresha yawned out.

"I'm so glad you're okay. How are you feeling?" Dominique asked.

"My head hurts, but I'm okay," Patresha answered.

"I knew you would make it," Miles said as he hugged his sister-in-law.

"Thanks, Miles." Patresha cracked a weak smile.

Next to come into the room were Dana and Neil. "Hi Patresha," Dana greeted.

"Hi Ms. Dana," Patresha greeted back.

"You gave us quite a scare young lady." Dana hugged Patresha. "I'm so glad you're okay."

"Thanks," Patresha said.

Endz walked in and greeted Patresha with a bouquet of Get Well Soon flowers and placed them on the side of her bed. "Hi, little lady."

"Mr. Washington. What are you doing here?" Patresha was pleasantly surprised.

"I had to check on my intern and people," Endz said with a smile. "You know you mean a lot to my little cousin and his wife here."

"That's right!" Dominique exclaimed. "And that mother-fucker better not run into me!"

"That's right because we will fuck them up!" Miles added.

"Hey girl!" Lexus greeted Patresha.

"Lexus!" Patresha lit up with excitement at the sight of her ride or die.

"I'm so glad you're okay!" Lexus hugged Patresha tight.

"Yeah, it was a close call," Wyatt said.

"Don't you be scaring us like that?" Be-vo said.

"Sorry, Be-vo." Patresha let out a little giggle.

"You get well soon, okay," Wyatt said.

"Okay, Wyatt."

"Hi Mr. Washington," Lexus greeted Endz.

"Hi, Lexus. Hey, Wyatt." Endz gave Wyatt dap. He turned to Be-vo. "Hey, Bellamy! Nice to see you again." He gave Be-vo dap.

"You know Mr. Washington?" Patresha asked Be-vo.

"I applied for his scholarship program and got accepted." Be-vo turned to Endz. "Thanks, Mr. Washington."

"No need to thank me. You earned it." Endz loved the way this young man thinks. He was impressed with the future DJing shrink.

"You okay, baby?" Neil asked Dana and pulled her close to him.

"I'm good. I'm just glad Patresha is gonna be okay." Dana turned to Patresha and said. "You rest dear."

"Yes, Ms. Dana."

"You rest easy and stay strong," Neil said to Patresha.

"Thanks, Neil," Patresha responded unenthusiastically doubting if he really meant it and showing up here all over Dana didn't help his case.

Neil noted Patresha's tone and it made him feel some type of way. He then turned to Dana. "You sure you okay, baby?"

"Yes, Neil. I'm fine." Dana was touched by Neil's concern for her. If only she knew his ulterior motive at that very moment.

Neil kissed Dana with deep passion right in front of Patresha to get a rise out of her. "Let's get some air. I need to make sure that my woman and my baby are good and comfy."

"Alright." Dana followed Neil out of the room.

Lexus, Wyatt, and Be-vo saw the broken look on Patresha's face and the three had the same exact thought about Neil because they knew what the fuck he was trying to pull with that stunt. *Fucking bastard!*

Dana was cuddled in Neil's arms on the couch in the waiting room. His phone started to ring, and he got off the couch. "I gotta take this. I'll be right back."

"I'll be right here," Dana said and Neil took his leave.

Dana sat quietly lost in her thoughts. She was glad Patresha was gonna be fine. She had other things on her mind like the baby and Neil's turnaround.

"How you doing?" Endz interrupted Dana's thoughts and took a seat next to her.

"I'm good. Thanks for checking on me," Dana said. "Crazy, isn't it? Who would do something like this to a sweet girl like Patresha?"

"I don't know but whoever the fuck it is they made a huge mistake. Believe that shit!" Endz meant business.

"You haven't changed a bit." Dana shook her head and laughed.

"You know how I get down," Endz reminded.

"I know," Dana said. She and Endz were deep in conversation with all smiles being observed by Lexus, Wyatt, and Be-vo.

"It's nice to see Mr. Washington smiling and laughing," Lexus said. "Sometimes he looks sad when I see him."

"Maybe he's lonely," Wyatt guessed.

"That's part of it," Be-vo said.

"What do you mean?" Lexus asked.

"Let's just say that some men are sad and lonely because the woman they want is with another man. Especially to a man that is undeserving."

"Oh, I see." Lexus knew what Be-vo was talking about.

"You did a great job, baby girl," Neil said on the call in a secluded area.

"Thank you," a woman's voice said. "Anything for you, baby. What's going on?"

"That fat bitch just woke up and don't worry, I'll buy you a new ride. Your choice," Neil promised.

"Thanks, Neil."

"You're welcome, Sarina."

Jamila

Chapter 17
2006

Things were going great in ten-year-old Dana's life in Atlanta, Georgia. She loved her school, friends, and her beautiful new house. Her mother, Veronica, was happily remarried to a nice successful man named Roman Murphy. Also, her brother, Eli, was a happy newlywed to a nice, beautiful, young lady who was attending Spelman College named Ant and Endz was enjoying college life at Morehouse College.

Dana was sleeping like a baby in her princess themed decorated bedroom all cuddled up with her stuffed pink dinosaur.

Boom!

Dana's peaceful slumber was interrupted by an earth-shattering door slam.

"Lando! What are you doing here? Get out now!" Dana heard Veronica yell out. Lando? Dana never thought she would ever hear that name again. How did he find them?

"You think you can just walk away from me like that! Huh bitch!" Lando yelled.

"Lando, it's over! I've moved on. Please leave! How did you find us anyway?" Veronica was beyond terrified.

"Don't worry about all of that! You running around with some nigga and got him around my kids!"

"Roman is my husband now! We are done and you have no one to blame but yourself! Now get the fuck over it and get the fuck out!"

Lando was pissed. He felt humiliated. His wife took his kids and left. To add insult to injury, she replaced him with another man. Lando was not gonna take that shit lying down. He had to find them ASAP and take back what was his. "I want my family back! Now get your shit and bring your ass home!" he demanded.

There was no way Veronica was going back to her abusive ex-husband and judging by his behavior he hasn't changed one bit. *"And you wonder why I left your ass! I'm calling the police!"* Veronica yelled.

"Bitch, you ain't calling nobody!"

"Lando get the fuck off of me!"

"Bitch!"

"Lando please stop!"

"Bitch shut the fuck up!"

The screaming and crashing sounds were all too familiar to Dana. She was terrified. Dana took a peek out the window and saw Roman's white Mercedes parked outside. Dana found it odd that Roman's car was outside, but he hasn't barged in here to save her momma.

Dana put on her bedroom slippers and quietly walked out of the house. She ran straight to the car to see if Roman could help her. She opened the passenger door and covered her mouth to hold in the scream at the sight of her stepfather's beaten and lifeless corpse in the driver's seat.

Dana didn't know what to do. Then she remembered Roman kept a cell phone in his pocket. She carefully reached inside his pants pocket and grabbed the phone. She dialed 911 and ran across the street and hid in the bushes.

"9-1-1, what is your emergency?" the emergency operator greeted.

"Please help me!" Dana pleaded. *"My daddy is hurting my momma and I think he killed my stepdaddy. I found him dead and beat up in his car. I found his cell phone to call you and now I'm in the bushes across the street! I'm so scared!"*

"I'm so sorry little girl. What's your name and how old are you?" the operator asked in a sweet voice.

"Dana Spicer. I'm ten years old."

"Okay baby, we're gonna help you. We're gonna send a police officer there right away sweetheart. What's your address?" Dana gave the operator the information. *"Thank you, baby. Just stay hidden until the police get there and stay on the phone with me okay."*

"Okay." Dana remained hidden while keeping an eye out for

*the police. Then she saw the front door opened. "Oh my God!"
She gasped.*

*"What's going on?" The operator asked with a deep
concern for the brave little girl wishing she was there to protect
her.*

*"My daddy is walking out of the house. His clothes are
covered with blood and he's unzipping his pants." Little Dana
reported as she trembled with fear. "I'm still in the bushes."*

*"Good girl! Just stay there until the police get there. You are
doing great! You are a brave little girl," the operator said. "Do
you see what's going on now?"*

*"Yes," Dana answered. "My daddy is going in my stepdaddy
Roman's car. He pushed him out and drove away." Dana told
the operator exactly what she saw. A few minutes later she saw a
bunch of police cars coming to the house. They got out of their
cars and surrounded the house. They covered Roman's dead
body with a black tarp. "The police are here!"*

*"Alright, baby! Just go up to one of them and they'll help
you, okay!"*

"Okay. Thank you and goodbye!"

"You're welcome, baby, and goodbye!"

*When the call ended, Dana got out of the bushes and slowly
approached the house. She was stopped by a beautiful dark-
skinned policewoman with fancy, straight-back cornrow braids.
"Hello, little girl! You're Dana, right?"*

*Dana nodded her head. "My momma is in there. I'm
scared."*

*"It's gonna be alright, sweetheart," the policewoman said,
hugging the frightened and traumatized little girl in her arms.
"We're gonna keep you safe."*

*Dana felt safe and secure with this nice lady. She saw the
EMT's come out carrying her now-deceased mother on a
stretcher with her naked, beaten, and sexually violated body
covered. The sight of her mother's dead body broke Dana down
completely. All she could do was scream and cry. "Momma! No!
No!"*

*****

"Aaah!" Dana woke up screaming her lungs out after dreaming about the night her father killed her mother and stepfather. The screaming continued 'til Endz barged into the room and pulled her into his arms.

"Dana! Dana!" Endz rocked Dana in his arms. "It's okay! I'm here! I'm here!" He let Dana cry in his arms.

When Dana calmed down a bit, Endz helped her get out of bed and helped her into his room. He helped her in his bed and made sure she was comfortable. "There you go. You relax and I'll be right back."

Endz walked out of the room and left Dana in his room. She hasn't had that nightmare in years. For years, she tried to desperately forget about that terrible night. To take her mind off that dream she let her body experience the comfort of this California King sized bed Endz got, She felt like she was laying on a cloud. *I got to get me one of these!* She thought.

"Here you go." Endz came back with two ice-cold bottles of water and handed Dana one.

"Thanks, Endz." Dana took the bottled water and opened it to take a sip.

"Anytime. What's wrong, baby girl?" Endz asked while drinking water.

"Had that nightmare again," Dana answered with a yawn. "It's weird. I haven't had that nightmare in years. I felt like I was right there again."

"The night of your mom's murder?" Endz guessed.

"Yeah."

"You still haven't visited your dad?"

"Fuck no!" Dana spat out with bitterness. Lando is doing life in prison for the murders thanks to the powerful testimony of his own ten-year-old daughter.

"Understandable." Endz nodded his head in agreement.

"The last time I saw him was at Eli's funeral. He tried to talk

110

to me, but I didn't wanna hear what the fuck he was trying to talk about."

"I'll never forgive that nigga!" And Dana meant that shit. She will forever hate that man for the permanent damage he has done to their family. After the murders, Dana moved in with Eli and Ant and they took care of her for the rest of her childhood.

As Dana cried, Endz pulled her into his arms. "It's okay, baby girl. He can't hurt you anymore." They laid there in absolute silence listening to the rain beginning to pour down. "Dana," he broke the peaceful silence.

"Yes, Endz?"

Endz sat up and looked Dana in her beautiful eyes. "I want you to always remember that you're completely safe with me, okay? I will never let anybody hurt you. Do you understand me?"

"Yes, Endz. I do."

"You are a special woman and I know I can trust you. But the question is, do you trust me?"

"Of course, I do."

"Alright."

It felt good for Dana to have Endz back in her life. If it wasn't for him, she wouldn't have the guts to stand up to Neil and put her foot down. She had to stand firm on him putting an end to his abusive and cheating ways. "Since we're trusting each other, can I ask you something?"

"Sure thing, baby girl."

"Why did you have to live with Momma Flo?" Dana asked with curiosity hoping that Endz would open up to her.

Endz looked at Dana and sighed. It was difficult to talk about, but he will for Dana. While his mother, Pearl, was pregnant with him, she found out his father was cheating on her. She broke off the engagement. He moved on with the woman who he was cheating with and abandoned his responsibilities as a father. He and his mistress turned main chick died in a car accident when Endz was ten months old.

Pearl then met a new man when Endz was four. She thought

she met the man of her dreams. That was until his wife confronted both of them on the street with a gun. The cowardly fuck nigga used his momma as a human shield and his wife turned the gun on herself. This happened right in front of five-year-old Endz.

After hearing Endz's tragic tale, Dana's heart broke for him. Having his mother taken from him right before his eyes at such a young age because of a ball-less, selfish, cheating ass nigga that wanted to have his cake and eat it too and didn't have the balls to take the first bullet. "I'm so sorry."

"It's okay, baby girl." Endz sighed as he rubbed the tattoo on the left side of his chest that resembled a pearl and on the inside it read 'R.I.P. Momma'. "I don't know where I'd be without grandma. I wish momma was here to see how Miles and I turned out. She was really crazy about Miles. She loved being an aunt." Endz rolled over to grab his phone that was on the dresser and scrolled through the pictures. "Check this out."

Dana looked at the picture with Pearl and Endz hugging and next to them was Ruby holding baby Miles in her arms. There was another picture of Pearl holding Miles. There was another picture of Momma Flo with both her daughters and both her grandsons. "Y'all look so happy and beautiful."

"Thank you. The rain sounds like it's starting to pick up," Endz said and put his phone back up. "Now, let's go to sleep and no more nightmares." He gently tapped Dana's nose. "If you have another one, I'll have to tickle you."

Dana sat up and looked at Endz up and down. "Oh really?"

"Hell yeah!"

"Nigga please!" Dana grabbed a pillow and hit Endz in the face with it, then threw it at him.

Endz caught the pillow in midair. "Oh, so it's like that?"

"Yeah, nigga? It's like that!" Dana playfully challenged Endz.

"Okay then! It's on!" Endz grabbed a pillow and hit Dana with it. She grabbed another pillow and they started having a pillow fight. They were laughing and hitting each other with pillow like they were kids. Dana threw another pillow at Endz and he ducked.

Dana pounced on top of him and started tickling his stomach making him laugh. "Yeah, nigga! Talk that shit now! Talking about you gonna tickle me!"

"Okay! Okay, you got me!" Endz surrendered and Dana backed off. He took the opportunity to gain the upper hand and tickle Dana like he and Eli used to gang up on her when she was little. "Yeah, you thought you got me!"

"Okay! Okay!" Dana laughed. "Okay! Okay! We're even!"

"Good!" Endz said as she caught his breath. The two giggled at how silly and childish they were acting until they fell asleep.

Jamila

Chapter 18

Meanwhile on the other side of town...

"Oh shit, girl! I'm about to nut!" Neil had Patresha flat on her back with her legs in the air in the back of his black Audi Q7 SUV.

"Aaah!" Patresha came as she was taking the rough dick.

After a few more aggressive pumps, Neil busted a huge nut inside her pussy. "Shit your pussy is great!" Neil breathed out with satisfaction and kissed Patresha.

"Thanks." She blushed as she and Neil got dressed.

As soon as Neil got dressed, he climbed in the front seat to take his place in the driver's seat. He started the car and took off while Patresha was still in the backseat getting dressed. "I gotta make a stop real quick," he said to Patresha.

"Okay," Patresha said. She appreciated how nice Neil was to her since the attack. He's been very sweet and compassionate. Just like the man she fell in love with at the party. He also stopped making fun of her weight. He promised to take her out on a romantic dinner tonight. First, he wanted to make love to her, and he couldn't wait so they parked at an abandoned park.

Patresha was hoping that Neil's business stop wouldn't take long so they can continue their date. Neil parked the car in front of some house and got out of the vehicle. Patresha watched him walk to the front door and rang the doorbell. A woman answered the door. Neil gave her a hug and kiss, then escorted her outside.

Patresha couldn't believe this shit. He opened the car door for her and helped her inside the passenger seat. Neil got back in the driver's seat and drove off. Patresha fumed on the inside for about five minutes before she finally spoke up. "Neil!"

"What?" he barked.

"What is she doing here?"

"I'm taking her out to eat," he answered nonchalantly.

"We had a date!" Patresha yelled. "And there's also something you need to know. This is the bitch that attacked me and put me in the hospital!"

"I see," Neil responded with a no big deal shrug and Sarina giggled finding the whole situation funny as fuck.

Neil's attitude towards this information was downright cruel. Not to mention the way he was showing too much public display of affection to Dana in Patresha's face right next to her hospital bed. Suddenly, she came up with a painful humiliating conclusion.

"You told her to do it! How could you do this to me? You're a disgusting motherfucker! I'm calling the police right motherfucking now to report you and this hoe ass bitch!" Patresha had it with Neil's disrespectful shit. She was not gonna let him get away with it. Not this time. She pulled out her phone to call 911.

Hearing the word police was making Sarina a little nervous and it showed all over her face. "Don't worry Sarina. I got this," Neil said to ease her worries.

Patresha dialed 911 and waiting for an answer. "9-1-1, what's your emergency?" The operator greeted.

"I..." Patresha couldn't get all of her words out because Neil dragged her out of the car causing her to hang up on the operator by accident.

"You call the cops and you're a dead, fat bitch! Do you motherfucking understand me?" Neil threatened.

"You sent her after me!" Patresha screamed as she pointed at a smug Sarina.

"She didn't even hit you that hard," he dismissed like Patresha ending up in the hospital and being knocked unconscious wasn't shit.

"I ended up in the hospital and my car was totaled!"

"But did you die?"

Is this nigga for real? "What?"

"You needed to learn a lesson about disrespecting me and obviously your fat ass didn't learn shit!" Neil looked back at Sarina who was still sitting in the car and motioned his head like he was telling her to come over here. She got out of the car and walked over to stand next to Neil. He turned his attention back to Patresha. "Now get on your knees and apologize to Sarina for calling her out of her name and scaring her."

Patresha scoffed and rolled her eyes "Fuck that bitch! Her ass is the one that owes..."

Patresha was cut off by a hard slap in the face by Neil. "Nobody owes you shit, bitch! I said get on your motherfucking knees!"

Patresha was terrified as fuck. She was standing in front of two of the most dangerous and ruthless people she has ever encountered. Her abusive lover and his side hoe that he recruited to almost kill her to send a message. Out of fear for her life, she got on her knees and faced Sarina. She began her coerced apology, "I'm sorry."

"For what?" Neil mocked.

"I'm sorry for calling you out of your name and scaring you."

"Ms. Smith," Neil wanted Patresha to add.

"Ms. Smith."

"And..."

"And I'm sorry for disrespecting you, Neil." Patresha just wanted this humiliating moment to be over with but Neil was not done yet.

"I don't think you're sorry enough," Neil said. "I think you need more time to think about your insolence." Neil and Sarina turned to walk towards the car. "Maybe the long walk back might clear your empty ass head and maybe you'll lose a couple of pounds while you're at it!" he yelled out as he and Sarina entered the car while laughing at Patresha like the cruel heartless monsters they were and drove away.

Patresha was left still on her knees all alone feeling lower than she has ever been in her life and that's saying a lot and to add insult to injury the rain was starting to fall.

Jamila

Chapter 19

Ring! Ring!

Lexus' phone interrupted her deep sleep. She was half awake as she reached for her phone and answered the call without checking to see who it was. "Hello!" she greeted with a yawn.

"Lexus! Can you please come get me?" Patresha begged.

The sound of Patresha in distress woke Lexus up completely. She figured she would be sleeping in her room not out somewhere at this hour. "Patresha? What's wrong? Where are you?" She was already out of the bed getting dressed.

"I'm at McDonald's on the corner of Slappy and Palmyra. My clothes are soaked. I've been walking for so long. I'm tired."

"Wait a minute. You were walking? From where?"

"Neil kicked me out of his car off Dawson Road."

"That nigga had you walking from Dawson Road to the corner of Slappy and Palmyra at this time of night." Lexus looked out the window and saw the rain pouring down. "In this weather?"

Lexus wanted to kill that motherfucker. She also wanted to know what the fuck was Patresha doing with that nigga in the first place. That was the question. "I thought you was done with that nigga!"

Patresha sighed. "It's a long story."

"Well, I'm about to jump in the car and come get you right now," Lexus said. "You just sit tight and when we get back to the apartment, you're gonna tell me everything motherfucking thing and don't leave shit out."

"Okay."

*****

"Thank you so much for picking me up. I'm so sorry I ruined your sleep." Patresha was deeply grateful to Lexus. They were back in their on-campus apartment with their food from McDonald's.

"Fuck all of that. You're my girl. If you need to be rescued from the bottom of the motherfucking ocean, I'm gonna be right there under that motherfucker!"

Patresha went into her room to change out of her soaking wet clothes into her warm and dry pajamas. Lexus changed into her pajamas and fixed two cups of hot chocolate. The two young ladies sat in the living room enjoying their food and hot chocolate.

"Alright Patresha, now that we're all settled in eating and shit, tell me everything. How did you end up walking in the rain in the middle of the night?" Lexus asked.

Patresha told Lexus every single detail about her relationship with Neil. From how he treated her to every single hurtful thing he has ever said and done to her.

"Patresha, you need to report his ass to the cops! That nigga is a fucking psycho!" Lexus knew Neil was a fuckboy, but she never imagined anything like this.

"No! No police!" Patresha shook her head. "He said he'll kill me if I told the cops. I'm probably in danger right now. I wasn't even supposed to tell you."

"Girl, that nigga is escalating. He needs to be dealt with." Lexus took a deep breath and came up with an alternative. "If you're not gonna press charges, at least stop fucking with him. The longer you deal with his ass the worse it's gonna get."

"But he said he loves me," Patresha cried. "He says he's sorry and he wouldn't do these things if I didn't push him and if I wasn't so fat…"

"You are buying right into his manipulating bullshit!" Lexus had to squash this ridicules nonsense Patresha was talking. "He's only saying this shit to control you. He knows exactly what to say and do to get to you and you keep giving him that power. You need to stop that shit. The only way you're gonna beat him is to not deal with his ass anymore."

Lexus shook her head and sighed. "You need to talk to somebody about this. Maybe you should tell your mother," she suggested.

"You know me and Dominique don't fuck with our momma. Especially Dominique."

"Oh yeah." Lexus almost forgot.

Patresha and Dominique's mother was a bitter woman who took it out of her daughters. Dominique's father left before she was born. Years later, their mother married Patresha's father. When Patresha was two, he divorced their mother to be with another woman. Ever since then she blamed her daughters for everything that went wrong in her life. Dominique especially.

"I know your mom is dead, but at least she loved you," Patresha said.

"Yes, she did," Lexus said. "Not a day goes by that I don't think about her."

Lexus' mother was a happily married woman with two children. Lexus and her older brother, Bryce. She was an accountant for a successful company. Her boss was always hitting on her. He was such a nasty ass fuck. He ignored her when she told him over a hundred times that she had no interest in him and that she was happily married with children. He also didn't give a shit about her being married with a family, let alone him being married with a family himself.

One day, he tried to force himself on her. Lexus' mother fought him off and screamed for help. Fortunately for her, the senior vice president was visiting the company that day and heard her screams. He barged in and came to her rescue. When it was all said and done, he fired the boss.

Things were back to normal. One day, nine-year-old Lexus and her mom went grocery shopping. After leaving the store, they headed for the car. Right there in the parking lot, her former boss, who unbeknownst to them was stalking her and the family, snatched her up, and kidnapped her leaving little Lexus behind. That was the last time she saw her mother alive. Her body was found in a ditch a week later beaten, tortured, and raped. Meanwhile, the whole terrible ordeal was videotaped and photographed.

Because of what happened and Lexus' mother was one of

the most valuable employees of the company, the senior vice president wanted to do something for the family. He tripled her life insurance policy for Lexus's father. He also set up scholarships and trust funds for Lexus and Bryce. Their trust funds couldn't be touched until they turned twenty-five years old.

"Maybe it's not too late for you and your mom to patch things up." Lexus hoped for Patresha.

Patresha scoffed and let out a sarcastic giggle. "You know even though momma acts like I don't even exist, I have a better chance at reconciling with momma than Dominique. Now those two really went at it." She turned to Lexus. "Thank you for being my friend."

"Of course, girl!" Lexus got out of her seat and walked over to put her arms around Patresha. "Thank you for being my friend too. I'm going to Miami to spend time with my family. Why don't you join me?"

"Really?"

"Yes really. Daddy already said it was okay. You can ride with me and Wyatt," Lexus said.

"Okay, I'll ride with y'all." Patresha accepted the invitation. She could use a vacation anyway. "Can we check out the University of Miami campus? I was thinking about checking out their Masters of Business Administration program."

"See, you're getting into the spirit already." Lexus smiled. "You're already planning your life without that bitch nigga already."

"Right. I'm done with his ass for real this time." Patresha was dead ass serious. That shit Neil pulled was the last motherfucking straw. There was no coming back from sending one of his hoes to try to kill her.

"Good."

"You know who I really feel sorry for?"

"Who?"

"Ms. Dana and that baby." Patresha kicked herself for believing anything that came out of Neil's lying ass mouth. Why in the fuck did she let Neil convince her that Dana was a terrible person? She was really a sweet and caring woman. She was a good friend to her sister and she even came to the hospital to see if she was okay. Neil's cruel ass only came to the hospital with Dana to be on some petty shit. Neil doesn't deserve Dana or to be a father. As far as Patresha was concerned Neil and that Sarina bitch deserve each other and Dana and that baby are better off without his ass.

"Ms. Dana has no idea what kind of man Neil really is," Patresha said with pity.

"We can only hope that she finds out before it's too late," Lexus said.

"So, do I Lexus. So do I."

Jamila

Chapter 20

"Mmmm! Mmmm" Neil and Dana were kissing passionately on the couch of her office. "I have a surprise for you," Neil said and gave Dana another kiss.

"Oooh wee! A surprise for me? What is it?" Dana was all smiles.

"Close your eyes."

"Okay." Dana closed her eyes.

It was under a minute for Neil said. "Okay, open them."

Dana opened her eyes and saw Neil on bended knee with an opened jewelry box in his hand revealing a huge diamond ring. It was bigger and had more bling than the engagement ring she was wearing now.

"Neil, what are you doing?" Dana was baffled.

"Dana, I love you. I know I haven't been the man you deserve in the past. I'm sorry for the pain and suffering that I put you through. You are the most beautiful and amazing woman in the world. I want to build a wonderful life and family with you. I will spend the rest of my life showing you how much you mean to me. Dana, will you give me the honor and privilege of being my wife?" Neil proposed.

"Didn't we already do this?" Dana was confused.

"Yes, I know but I'm proposing to you again because I want us to start over with a clean slate. That's what this new engagement ring symbolizes. A new beginning for us," Neil explained.

Dana looked at Neil and soaked in the gesture. She sighed and before opening her mouth. "If I say yes do you promise to love and cherish me? Do you promise to be a good father to our child and any future children we might have? And to also be faithful, respectful, and not be abusive towards me in any way, shape, or form and continue to go to your therapy?"

"Yes, baby. I promise." Neil kept up with his rehearsed speech and tricks.

"Yes, Neil. I will marry you...again!" Neil and Dana busted

out laughing at her answer.

"That's my girl!" Neil took off Dana's previous engagement ring and replaced it with the new one. Neil proceeded to join Dana on the couch and the two kissed to celebrate their renewed engagement.

Knock! Knock!

"Come in!" Dana said to whoever was knocking at the door and gave Neil a final kiss.

"Hi, Ms. Dana." Lexus let herself inside the office.

"Hi, Lexus! How are you?" Dana greeted.

"I'm doing good."

"Hey, Lexus!" Neil greeted with his charm.

"Hi," Lexus politely greeted. She did a great job hiding her disgust at the sight of this evil bastard.

"Ms. Dana, here's the file for your business trip." Lexus handed Dana the file.

"Thank you so much," Dana said as she grabbed the file. "You know you and Patresha have been a great help to me and the company. It's interns like you that keep this company running. I know for a fact that you and Patresha will make brilliant business partners in the future."

"Wow! Thank you, Ms. Dana!" Lexus blushed. "You are such a sweet lady. You deserve a good and wonderful man."

"She sure does." Neil put his arms around Dana and kissed her. "And she's got one right here."

I wasn't talking about your ass, nigga! Lexus wanted to scream in Neil's face. "Ms. Dana, is there anything else you need from me today?"

"No there isn't. I'm about to head out in a few minutes. Thanks for everything," Dana said. "You, Wyatt, and Patresha have a good time on your trip and be safe."

"We will," Lexus said. "And you be safe too."

"Thanks and tell Patresha that I hope she feels better," Dana said as Lexus took her leave.

"What's this about a trip?" Neil asked in fake curiosity trying to get information. He didn't want his low self-esteem having, overweight, mistress getting any ideas trying to break up with him while she's away or runs her mouth about their business too much. He feels like women be on some bullshit when they travel by themselves. Or hunting for random dick. Even if they travel for business.

"Oh, I gotta go to New York for a business trip and after that, I'm gonna stop in Atlanta to visit Ant. My niece is having a piano recital and I promised her I'd be there," Dana explained.

"I see." Neil wasn't interested in Dana's plans. He saw he had to use a different approach. "What's wrong with Lexus' friend?" he asked like he had a fucking heart.

"Oh, Patresha? I'm not sure, but Lexus said she's been down lately and hopefully this family trip to Miami she invited Patresha on cheers her up," Dana shared.

"I'm sure it will," Neil said. *Miami! That's worse than I thought!* Miami and any beautiful warm climate cities bring out the hoe in women as far as he was concerned.

"That girl has been through so much." Dana sighed. "I still can't believe somebody would have so much hate in their heart to attack a sweet innocent girl like Patresha."

"You got me." Neil played it off like he had no clue.

"Right." Dana sighed. "Well, I'm about to head out."

"You thought about my question?" Neil asked.

Dana knew exactly what question that was. "About me moving back in with you?"

"I really miss you." Neil sounded like he was about to cry. This nigga was going all out. "I miss holding you and making love to you. I miss waking up next to your sweet beautiful sexy self."

"I know I've been putting it off." Dana knew she had to give her answer sooner or later so she came up with an idea. "I'll think about it and when I get back, I'll give you my answer. Deal?"

"Deal."

Jamila

Chapter 21

"This place is beautiful!" Patresha was in awe of the beautiful city of Miami, Florida. She was sitting in the backseat with Wyatt behind the wheel and Lexus sitting by his side in the passenger seat.

"Yes, it is!" Lexus agreed.

"I can't wait to check out the campus," Patresha said.

"Where are we staying?" Wyatt asked Lexus.

"With my brother, Bryce, and his wife, Aiesha," Lexus answered. "There's plenty of room at their house."

"Who's gonna give us a tour of the campus?" Patresha asked.

"My cousin, Chase Roberts," Lexus said. "He's a nurse and does some CNA work on the side. In fact, that's the reason we're in Miami. To celebrate his twenty-third birthday."

"Chase is good people," Wyatt said. They found the beautiful and prestigious campus of The University of Miami.

"Yes, he is. Chase is my nigga! We're like this!" Lexus crossed her fingers as Wyatt tried to find somewhere to park.

"Would you consider living here?" Patresha asked Lexus.

"Yes, I would." Lexus turned to Wyatt and asked. "What about you?"

"You know wherever you go, I'll go." Wyatt kissed Lexus' hand. "Besides, with all of the parties and rappers having concerts and shit here, I can make some good money."

"And Be-vo could make good money here too," Patresha said. "Too bad he couldn't join us."

"Why not?" Wyatt said.

"His sisters had a basketball game at their high school, and he wanted to check it out," Patresha said.

"He loves those girls." Lexus admired Be-vo's dedication to his   little   sisters.

"Here we are." Wyatt found a parking space and the three got out of the car.

"Where's Chase? He should be here," Lexus wondered.

"Yoo-hoo! Princess Alexandria!" a handsome, chocolate skinned, young man with a six-foot muscular frame and his neat shoulder-length dreadlocks that were pulled in a ponytail called out. He approached the group looking all sexy in his navy-blue scrubs.

"Chase!" Lexus jumped into her big cousin's arms and planted a big kiss on his cheek. "How are you? I missed you!"

"I missed you too, baby girl! I'm good! Wyatt, what's up man?" Chase gave him dap. "You taking care of my baby cuz here?"

"Of course." Wyatt pulled Lexus close to him. "This my queen right here."

"Chase, here's my best friend, Patresha Glover. Patresha, this is my cousin, Chase," Lexus introduced.

"So, you're Patresha. I've heard a lot about you." Chase pulled Patresha into a hug. *He smells so good!* Patresha thought. "So glad to finally meet you, friend."

"Friend?" Patresha was confused. She's just meeting this dude and he's calling her a friend.

"Yes. Any friend of Lexus is a friend of mine." Chase flashed his perfect smile.

"Are you excited about turning twenty-three?" Patresha asked.

"Very excited," Chase answered and walked everybody over to the tour cart. "Well let's get the tour started. Y'all hop in."

Chase got behind the wheel of the tour cart and everybody else climbed in and buckled up before he took off. He gave a thorough tour of the campus. Explained the history. He showed them The University of Miami Hospital which is where he worked. After the tour Chase took them to eat lunch at the student center.

"This place is huge. I can't wait to go to school here," Patresha said.

"Girl, this is just the campus. Wait 'til you get the tour to the city," Chase said.

"We get all of that on the first day?" Wyatt asked.

"Yes, you do. After we leave here, y'all can get settled in at Bryce's house. After, y'all get the tour of the city and check out my new condo." Chase laid out the itinerary.

"Wow! A black Mercedes truck and a condo. You must be really getting the bag." Patresha was impressed. After the tour of the campus, Chase let them check out his black Mercedes truck before lunch. He let Patresha ride shotgun and Lexus and Wyatt sit in the back on their way to the student center.

"Yep, I grew with the mentality you don't work, you don't eat," Chase said.

"Exactly!" Lexus chimed in. "Granddaddy taught us well."

"How are you and Lexus cousins?" Patresha asked.

Chase pointed at Lexus. "Her and Bryce's mom, Aunt Colleen, and my dad are brother and sister. Lexus and Bryce were like brother and sister to me because I'm the only child in my family. Lexus and I are closer in age which explains how tight we are."

"Do you like being a nurse?" Patresha asked.

"I love it." Chase nodded. "I always wanted to help people and make a difference in a small way. My mom is a nurse and my dad is a pharmacist. So, I guess you can say that I carried on the medical profession tradition so to speak."

Lexus looked at her text message. "Daddy is staying with Uncle Milo and Aunt Sadie. He's enjoying Uncle Milo's new man cave and Aunt Sadie let them have it by going shopping."

"I knew Uncle August would like dad's new man cave and you know how momma loves to shop." Chase chuckled. "Maybe I should stay with Bryce too with the rest of you guys. I don't wanna be all alone while y'all having a good time," he joked.

"Nigga, you're so silly!" Lexus playfully swatted Chase in the back of his head.

Chase turned his attention to his cousin's beautiful and sweet best friend. "So Patresha, how y'all enjoying college?"

"Great!" Patresha, Lexus, and Wyatt answered simultaneously.

"I know Lexus and Wyatt are going strong, but Patresha how

is your dating life?" Chase asked.

"A hot ass mess." Patresha sighed. She was deeply ashamed of herself for allowing herself to get caught up with an evil manipulating abusive bastard like Neil.

"I don't like the sound of that," Chase expressed his concern.

"Long story short, he did some terrible things to me. He called me names and fat-shamed me on a regular basis," Patresha recapped with gloom.

"He sounds like a bitch ass fuck nigga." Chase rolled his eyes and scoffed with disgust.

"You don't know the half of it," Lexus added.

"The important thing is that he's out of your life." Chase looked into Patresha's beautiful eyes and said with deep sincerity and care, "That nigga doesn't deserve a queen like you."

Patresha was blown away. "Queen? Me?"

"Yes girl, you!" Lexus encouraged.

"Don't tell me nobody has called you a queen before?" Chase found like hard to believe.

"Nope. You're the first," Patresha admitted.

"Shit! Patresha if you was my woman you would know how a queen is supposed to be treated. All day and every day," Chase said.

"Right," Wyatt said.

"Well, I've got to work tomorrow at my CNA gig. Why don't y'all tag along with me?" Chase invited.

"We'd love to, but daddy wanted to have breakfast and spend the day with me, Wyatt, Bryce, and Aiesha," Lexus said.

"Well Patresha, I guess it's gonna just be me and you. I'll try not to bore you too much," Chase joked which made Patresha laugh. *Love that smile! So sexy!* He thought.

"No never that," Patresha said. "I'd love to see you in action. And don't worry. If it gets too boring, I'll bring out my clown suit."

Everybody laughed. "Girl, you are a trip." Chase laughed.

Lexus and Wyatt had never seen this side of Patresha. She'd never been this relaxed, confident, and free around a man.

Into the Arms of His Boss

Maybe this could be the start of a beautiful new life for Patresha.

Jamila

Chapter 22

Everybody was sitting around in the living room at the home of the beautiful, thirty-three year old Antoinette Morris-Spicer in Atlanta, Georgia. After their successful business trip in New York, Dana, Endz, Dominique, and Miles stopped in Atlanta to spend a few days with Ant and her kids. Starting with watching Connie's piano recital that was at the Atlanta Botanical Garden.

"Good job, girl! You were amazing out there!" Dana congratulated her beautiful ten-year-old niece, Connie, who shared the same creamy peanut colored complexion, facial features, hazel eyes, and long curly light brown hair as her mother.

"Thanks, Aunt Dana," Connie said.

"Yeah, girl you killed it!" Dominique cheered.

"Thanks, Ms. Dominique." Connie blushed. "I was so nervous. It was my first solo. Momma told me to have courage and face my fears."

"And you did." Ant with her five-foot-four, one hundred and fifty pounds, thick in the right places frame held her mini-me tight and kissed her forehead. "That's my baby!"

Endz got out of his seat and Miles followed suit. "Well let's go fire up this grill," Endz said.

"Good because I'm hungry as hell!" Dominique rubbed her stomach.

"Uncle Nicky, will you teach me how to barbeque?" Eli Jr. asked.

"Boy, you too young to barbeque!" Ant chucked at her cute, brown-skinned, eight-year-old son who was the spitting image of her dearly departed husband.

"Your momma is right EJ, but you can come to watch us," Endz said.

"Yay!" EJ cheered and followed Endz and Miles outside into the patio.

"I'm gonna go in the entertainment room and practice," Connie told Ant.

"Okay baby," Ant said, and Connie went on her way.

"How you liking your presents Dana?" Ant asked as she walked into the dining room with Dana and Dominique following her.

"They're wonderful, Ant," Dana said as the ladies took their seats. "You didn't have to go through all the trouble."

"I wanted to," Ant insisted. "This is my future niece you're carrying." Ant couldn't help herself. She had to go all out shopping for Dana's unborn daughter.

"Thank you." Dana took a peek at the patio and saw EJ sitting in a chair observing Endz and Miles on the grill. She could also hear Connie practicing on the piano in the entertainment room. "I love those babies."

"Yeah. I see Eli in both of them every day." Ant never got over Eli's murder. He was her everything. If it wasn't for the kids, she might've ended up totally losing her fucking mind.

Dominique was very quiet. All this talk about babies and kids was making her feel some type of way. Before the trip, she was disappointed with another negative pregnancy test. Sometimes she felt hopeless. She and Miles wanted to be parents so badly, but she just couldn't get pregnant.

Dana looked over and noticed the spaced-out look on her best friend's face. "Dominique, are you okay?"

Dominique shook her head to erase her thoughts. "Oh, I'm fine. I just forgot something." She grabbed her phone to do something real quick. When she was done, she put her phone back up. "There we go."

"What did you forget?" Ant asked.

"I forgot to Cash App my baby sister, Patresha. She went on a trip with her friends to Miami," Dominique said.

"You know when I see you taking care of Patresha reminds me how Eli used to take care of me," Dana said. "He used to give me money when I was in college." She then grabbed Ant's hand and added, "Both of you looked after me and when Eli died, you still took care of me. Thank you."

"Anytime sweetie." Ant hugged Dana. "I was trying to do

what Eli would've done. He loved you and so do I."

"Yeah, Patresha is my baby right there!" Dominique glowed with pride and joy. Patresha was the closest she had to a child. Dominique didn't really have a choice but to be a parent to Patresha since their momma wasn't about shit.

"Did they ever find out who attacked her?" Dana asked.

"Fuck no!" Dominique snarled with disappointment.

"Somebody attacked that girl?" Ant was just now hearing about this. She wanted to know who in the fuck would attack an innocent college girl.

"Yes. I'm just glad she's okay," Dominique said with relief.

"I hope they catch that motherfucker!" Ant switched from being pissed off as fuck to being calm, cool, and collected while asking with a warm smile, "So, what do y'all have planned for tomorrow?"

"Well, Miles and Endz are going to a basketball game. I don't know what Dana and I are gonna do." Dominique shrugged her shoulders. "We haven't really made any plans."

"Well, y'all got plans now." Ant sprung on Dana and Dominique. "I'm going to a book signing and you two are coming with me."

"Okay cool." Dana went with the flow. "Who's the author?"

"She wrote this memoir I just finished entitled *Boss Chicks Don't Fold: Story of an Outside Child* by Thuy Mackenzie Ellis-Kilborn," Ant answered. She grabbed her tablet that was laying on the counter to show Dana and Dominique the book cover from her Amazon Kindle App. It was a picture of Thuy wearing a classic ivory dress and an ivory hat. Blinging diamond jewelry with black sunglasses and black stiletto heels sitting on the head of a black Audi with her legs closed while holding a football with both hands with the background covered with all types of sports equipment.

"That cover is sharp!" Dominique complimented. "She is so beautiful."

"Yes, she is!" Dana agreed. She took a closer look at Thuy's picture and her full name. "Wait a minute. I think I've seen her before and heard that name somewhere. But where?"

"Think hard. It'll come to you." Ant already knew the answer. In fact, that's why she wanted to read the book.

It took a minute for Dana's memory to refresh. "Now I remember! She was engaged to that baseball player who tried to have her and their unborn child killed."

"That's right," Dominique said. "He played for the Atlanta Braves. His name was Jeromy Fuller. She survived, but the baby didn't. That nigga was foul for doing that sick ass shit."

"I know right," Dana agreed. "What the fuck is wrong with people to have their minds take them there?"

"You got me." Ant was baffled. "Her story is crazy as fuck."

"Didn't her brother and sister steal a lot of money from her and the daddy knew about it?" Dana asked.

"That's right," Ant confirmed.

"That's fucked up!" Dominique shook her head with disgust.

"And if you think that's fucked up, in the book, she talks about how she found out she married her long-lost sister's ex-husband," Ant pointed out.

Dominique and Dana's eyes stretched with shock. "Excuse me!" They shrieked.

"I shit you not." Ant held up her right hand like she was taking a sacred oath. "Thuy found out had a long-lost sister and that long lost sister is the ex-wife of the dude Thuy is married to now."

"Damn!" Dana was blown away. She turned to Dominique and told her, "We gotta get this book and read it right now!" She went over to the side of the couch where she left her laptop bag and dug inside for her tablet so she could download the book.

"I'm on it," Dominique Sonic dashed to the guest room she shared with Miles, grabbed her tablet, and rejoined the ladies, and downloaded the book. "I've got so many questions for that chick when we go to that book signing tomorrow."

"Oh, honey, I already got my written down." Ant showed them the list of questions she'd written on a piece of paper and they all laughed.

138

Chapter 23

"I'm so glad to be off!" Chase cheered behind the wheel of his luxurious ride. He turned to face the beauty sitting next to him on the passenger seat. "I hope I didn't bore you too much."

"Nope!" Patresha flashed a smile. "I enjoyed myself. It was great seeing you in action. taking care of your patients."

"Just doing what I love," Chase said. "Hey, you did a great job too. The way you were keeping them company. You're a natural."

"Thanks." She blushed.

"You are beautiful with a beautiful heart," Chase complimented.

"And you are a sweet handsome man." Patresha couldn't believe a man was calling her beautiful. Not only was Chase calling her beautiful, but he actually meant that shit. "Do you really think I'm beautiful?"

"Of course. Why would you doubt that?"

"Because I'm not a size six and..."

"And what does that mean?" Chase interrupted. "Beauty comes in all different shapes and sizes. Besides, you have amazing curves. You have a very well proportionate shape." Chase admired Patresha's beauty, her face, smile, eyes, long jet-black hair, and her sexy shapely body.

"The men I've come across never thought that way. They pretended they did only to fuck in private. I guess that's all I'm good for. That's what Neil said," Patresha said with shame.

Patresha's phone started to ring and she dug in her purse to answer. She frowned at Neil's name on the caller ID. "Speak of the devil."

Chase saw Patresha move her finger to the ignore button and stopped her. "No, don't press ignore."

Patresha turned to Chase with her eyebrow raised. "Why not?"

"This is your first step to a new life," Chase explained. "Answer it and tell that nigga it's over."

Jamila

That wasn't part of Patresha's plan. Her plan was to ignore Neil and never see or speak to him ever again. She was never good with the direct approach, but with Chase by her side, she gained her courage. "Okay." She smiled at Chase and took a deep breath before answering the phone. *I have an idea! This nigga thinks he's the King of Pettiness! Two can play that game!* She gave Chase the shush signal and put it on speakerphone.

Without giving Patresha the chance to say hello, Neil went ahead and jumped right into his fake ass apologies and pleas. "Baby, I'm sorry for everything! I've been thinking about you..."

"Listen motherfucker, it's over!" Patresha was fed up with Neil and his lying and abusive ass. She wanted to make it crystal clear. Besides, she was in no mood to hear any of Neil's fake, whining bullshit.

This bitch nigga is pathetic! Chase covered his mouth to prevent a laugh from slipping out. He found Neil's fake ass crying stunt laughable.

"I'm done with your ass!" Patresha went all the way in on Neil's ass. "Don't call me no more! Don't text me no more! Stay the fuck away from me or I will tell the police, Ms. Dana, my sister, her husband, and his cousin everything!"

Did this bitch just threaten me? Neil thought. "You ungrateful, fat ass bi..."

Patresha officially closed that chapter in her life by hanging up in Neil's face. "Good job!" Chase congratulated. "How did that feel?"

"A-FUCKING-MAZING!" Patresha felt like a giant weight was lifted off her shoulders. Now, her life can truly begin. Finally, that horrible and humiliating living nightmare was over for good.

"Now that, that is taken care of, on to step two. Let a real man take you out on a date." Chase grabbed Patresha's hand and gently kissed her. "Will you do me the honor, Queen?"

"You wanna take me out on a date?" Patresha was really feeling Chase. She hoped he was sincere. He seemed to be so far.

"Of course."

140

Patresha still wasn't sure, but hey, going out on a date with Chase wouldn't hurt. Besides, he's Lexus' cousin. If he's anything like Lexus, Patresha figured she should be in safe hands with him. "Alright, I'll go out with you. If you promise not to try anything."

"What do you mean?" Chase didn't know what Patresha was referring to at first, but quickly got the point. "Oh, of course not. I wouldn't try you like that. Like I said. Lexus people are my people and I don't fuck over my people."

"Good to know." Patresha nodded.

"And I still have my V-card," Chase volunteered out of nowhere.

Did I hear him correctly? Patresha thought. "Run that by me again?"

"It's true?" Chase confirmed. "I'm still a virgin."

Patresha couldn't believe this shit. "Are you serious?"

"As a heart attack." Chase nodded his head.

"You mean to tell me that you almost twenty-three years old. Fine and sexy and you never had any pussy at all in your whole entire life?"

"Nope."

"Not even your dick sucked?"

"Nope." Chase shook his head. "No sexual contact with a woman whatsoever. I'm straight just in case you were wondering and I'm not on the down-low either." Chase knew being a virgin at his age would be a shocker to people. After revealing that fact sometimes, they wonder if he's gay. Nope Chase is completely straight.

"Never doubted that." Patresha knew Chase preferred pussy. He just never had it before. "Well, here we are." Chase parked at Bryce and Aiesha's driveway. Patresha was about to open the door to get out. "Hold on." He stopped her. He got out of the car. He went over to Patresha's side to open her car door. "Here you go."

What a gentleman! "Thanks!" Patresha was loving this new chapter of her life already.

Chase walked Patresha to the house and used his key to let her inside. "There you go. I'll be back," he said.

"Okay," Patresha said and she and Chase hugged before he headed out.

Patresha felt like she was on top of the world. She couldn't wait to share her good feeling with Lexus. "Lexus! Lexus, are you here!" Patresha called out as she went up the stairs.

"Yes!" Lexus yelled out from one of the guest rooms.

Patresha entered Lexus' guest room with a huge smile on her face. "Lexus guess what? Chase asked me out on a date. He is so sweet and the perfect gentleman."

"I know. Chase is solid." Lexus was happy for her best friend. "I'm so happy for you!" She gave Patresha a big hug. "How was your day?"

"It was great!" Patresha answered. "Oh, I almost forgot. On the way here guess who had the nerve to call me?"

"What the fuck did Neil want this time?" Lexus correctly guessed with an eye roll.

"You know his fuckboy ass was gonna call trying to feed me all that bullshit about him being sorry for dogging me out and it'll never happen again." Patresha waved off. "At first, I was gonna ignore him, but Chase encouraged me to answer and tell his ass off."

"You really told him off?" That was a hard thing for Lexus to picture but she's glad it happened.

"Yes, the fuck I did. I had his ass on speakerphone, so Chase could hear his fake ass 'baby, I'm sorry' begging and pleading bullshit. It took everything for us to hold in our laughter." Patresha giggled and Lexus joined in. "Oh, Lexus you should've been there. I tore that motherfucker a new one. I threatened to report his ass and tell Dominique and her people everything if he came anywhere near me again."

"You right. I should've been there." Lexus would've given anything to witness Patresha cancel Neil's ass. She was proud of the young woman Patresha was becoming and now she has a real man in her life.

142

"To be honest, I didn't think I had it in me," Patresha confessed. "But with Chase there encouraging me I felt invincible."

"That's what happens when you have a real man by your side," Lexus said. "I'm sure your date is gonna be amazing."

"I think so too." Patresha agreed. "That Chase is filled with surprises. He told me something very crazy and weird about himself."

"Oh, you mean about him still being a virgin?" Lexus blurted out.

Patresha stretched her eyes. "You know? Shit, y'all are super close!"

"We made a pact that if we were ever ready for our first time, we would consult each other and counsel each other to see if it was the right decision. We promised to tell each other after we did it," Lexus explained.

After hearing Lexus' explanation, Patresha came to a conclusion. "So that means Chase knows that you and Wyatt..."

"Yes, he does," Lexus admitted. "He gave me great advice. He wanted to make sure that I was comfortable and ready before taking me and Wyatt's relationship to that level."

Patresha wished she that type of wise male guidance in her life. Maybe it wouldn't have taken this long for her to get it right when it came to men. "You're lucky to have Chase in your life."

"Yes, I am and now he's in your life." Lexus put her arm around Patresha.

"How was your morning?" Patresha asked.

"Breakfast was great, and we visited one of momma's friends. We had a good time sharing fond memories."

Patresha noticed that Lexus was the only person in the house. "Where is everybody?"

Lexus leaned back in the bed. "Wyatt is with daddy and Bryce. Aiesha went to her momma's house. When she comes back, she's gonna take me to go shopping for Chase's birthday present."

"I need to figure that out too." Patresha turned to Lexus and asked, "Will you help me?"

"Sure. We'll go find something tomorrow." There was a knock at the door and Lexus yelled out. "Come in!"

"I'm back!" Chase entered the room and announced himself. He had two bouquets of red roses along with shopping bags from Nordstrom and Bloomingdales.

"Hey!" Lexus and Patresha greeted.

"Roses for the two lovely ladies." Chase gave Lexus and Patresha each a bouquet of roses.

"Thank you." Lexus blushed and hugged Chase.

"And here's something for my queen." Chase gave Patresha the shopping bags.

Patresha felt like a little kid on Christmas day. She took out the contents in the bags. In the bags were a pair of sparkling diamond earrings and an elegant black dress. "Wow! These are beautiful!"

"Just like you," Chase said. "You need something to wear for our date tonight."

"Shit girl! You got my cousin all sprung and shit!" Lexus giggled. "See, I told you! You got it, girl!"

"Thanks." Patresha blushed. She gave Chase a big hug. "Thank you so much!"

"But before we go out, I need you to do something," Chase said to Patresha.

"What's that?" Patresha asked.

"Call your sister."

"Okay." That was an odd request, but Patresha obliged. She dialed the number and waited for an answer.

"Hey, Patresha. What's up?" Dominique greeted.

"Hey, Dominique."

"Are you having a good time in Miami?"

"Yes, I am," Patresha answered with a smile which made Chase fall deeper for her. "Let me put you on Facetime." Patresha pressed the button and saw Dominique's face on the screen. "Hey, Dominique!"

"Look at my baby sister glowing like a motherfucker!"

Dominique loved seeing her beautiful baby sister happy.

"Hey, Dominique!" Lexus took a seat next to Patresha and greeted them.

"Hey, Lexus! How are you?"

"I'm great! Enjoying the Miami weather."

"I know girl! I need to make a trip back down there."

"Dominique, there's a reason I wanted to call you." Patresha motioned with her hand for Chase to approach her. He sat on the other side next to Patresha and she began the introduction. "Dominique, this is Chase Roberts. He's Lexus' cousin. His birthday is in two days. Chase, this is my sister, Dominique."

"Hello, ma'am! Nice to meet you!" Chase greeted.

"Boy, your ass ain't gotta call me ma'am. I'm not even thirty yet," Dominique chuckled. She knew he was being polite and showing manners, but the way this nigga saying ma'am almost had her turning around to see if her beloved grandmother was behind her, but remembered she was dead. "Happy early birthday by the way."

Chase went ahead to state the reason he wanted Patresha to call Dominique. "Well Dominique, the reason I wanted to talk to you is because your sister is a beautiful and special young lady. I would like to take Patresha out on a date to get to know her and build a relationship with her. If that's okay with you?"

Dominique was very impressed by this young man's respect. He actually wanted to ask her for permission to take her baby sister out. "Oh really?"

"Yes. Patresha told me how close you two are and how you took care of her. I felt it was only right to ask you for your permission," Chase said.

"I see you're a good-looking young man. What do you do for a living?" If this dude wanted to date Patresha, Dominique wanted to know every nook and cranny about him.

"I'm a nurse and I do some CNA work on the side," Chase answered.

"How old are you?"

"I'm about to turn twenty-three and I promise to treat your

sister with the utmost respect. Like the queen that she is."

He's close to my age and his ass was calling me some damn ma'am! Dominique thought. "Do you have any kids?"

"No, I don't have any children."

"Not even possibilities?" Dominique wanted to be extra sure.

"Oh, I'm positive," Chase said matter of factly.

"How can you be so sure?"

"Because I never had sex before."

The look on Dominique's face said it all. *Is this nigga serious?* Deep down she knew he was. "Really?"

"It's true, Dominique," Lexus defended. "Chase is a virgin."

Dominique sat in complete silence to think about all of this. It was a good three minutes before she gave her answer. "I see you are a real hard-working young man and you're making my sister smile and as long as you keep making her smile, we're good. You have my blessing," she gave her stamp of approval.

"Thanks, Dominique. And don't you worry, Patresha is in great hands," Chase assured her. "You have my word that you won't regret this."

"See that I don't," Dominique said. "Have a great time and happy early birthday."

"Thank you," Chase said.

"I love you, Dominique," Patresha said.

Dominique blew a kiss. "I love you too, baby girl."

Chapter 24

Endz and Miles were sitting in one of the exclusive suites at the State Farm Arena enjoying the Atlanta Hawks and Los Angeles Lakers basketball game. They were cheering and having a good time while the ladies went to the book signing and the kids were spending the day with Ant's mother. During halftime, the cousins were having a couple of beers and enjoying the luxuries of the suite.

"We need to bring EJ to the games with us sometime," Endz suggested. "His daddy loved basketball. I remember when Eli and I would be up here enjoying the games, balling out and shit. I wish he was here to enjoy all of this success. Without him, none of this would be possible." Endz was still in pain over his fallen best friend.

Miles only met Eli once when Endz brought him along during one of his visits to Fort Valley State University during the time Miles was a student. Endz used to drop in on Miles when he was living on Fort Valley's campus to either give him money or teach him the game. Eli seemed like a real dude to Miles and he was very loyal to Endz and vice versa. "That shoe store he built was great and it's still going strong thanks to you."

"Just keeping my homeboy's legacy alive," Endz said. "And looking after Ant, the kids, and Dana. I owe it to Eli to make sure they're straight."

"Speaking of Dana. When are you gonna quit being a pussy and get your woman? There, somebody had to say it," Miles blurted out what everybody else was thinking.

Endz gave his baby cousin a crazy look for even suggesting that shit. "Nigga, what are you talking about?" He thought Miles was out of his motherfucking mind.

"Uh, Dana..." Miles reminded. "Come on Endz, everybody knows there's something between y'all."

"Uh, yeah...friendship," Endz corrected. "Nothing like that is going on between me and Dana."

"Alright nothing has happened between y'all, but something

is going on." Miles wasn't letting up. "Y'all just don't know it and see it."

"I don't know what you talking about."

"Nicholas Milhouse Washington!" Miles playfully scolded his big cousin like he was a child. "Being in denial is not healthy!"

Endz stared up and down Miles real quick before giving his response. "You just gonna scream out my whole government like that lil nigga? You really wanna take it there, Kiriakis!"

Miles's eyes turned into slits when Endz blurted out his real first name. Miles hated his first name. There it was. His full name was Kiriakis Miles Cooper. "Touché nigga! Touché!" He gave Endz dap in respect of his get back. "So, back to you and Dana."

Endz shook his head. He never considered going there with Dana. "Dana is about to get married and she's carrying Neil's baby."

"I don't know if he's the one for her." Miles sounded doubtful. "Dominique had her suspicions about him since the party."

Now that got Endz attention. "What suspicions?"

"She thinks that Dana is hiding some things about Neil."

"You don't say." Endz nodded his head. "I'll be sure to keep my eyes opened."

"That's the spirit!" Miles patted Endz on the back. "Look after your woman!"

"Dana is not my woman!" Endz insisted with authority in his voice.

"Not yet."

"Look, even if I was interested in Dana in that way, I would never cross that line."

"What line?"

"She's Neil's fiancée and I don't go after another man's woman," Endz said. "Also, Eli wouldn't approve. That's his baby sister."

Miles sighed before giving his opinion. "Look, I don't know

about Eli, but I know he loved you and Dana. If he was alive, I think he would approve. As long as you and Dana were happy, and you were treating her right everything would be cool, right?"

"Right." Endz knew Miles made some sense.

Miles continued. "You got her living in your house to clear her head. She trusted you and feels safe with you. Now, how do you feel about her?"

"She's a sweet and beautiful special woman. Neil is lucky to have her."

"Hypothetically speaking, if Neil wasn't in the picture would you go after her?"

"Dana is very beautiful, attractive, and sexy. I will admit that." Endz smiled in admiration of Dana's inner and outer beauty.

"Oh shit! That's my nigga! I knew it!" Miles teased. "That's a start!"

"I'm a man, okay!" Endz stopped Miles' silly ass cheering. "Of course, I know a beautiful woman when I see one."

Miles decided to switch it up and be serious for a second. His big cousin deserved to be happy. He was tired of seeing him alone. Ever since Dana came back in Endz's life, he's become a different man. He was more alive. It was a great thing to see. "I tell you nothing is more amazing than having a loyal beautiful woman by your side. All day and all night. She's all yours and you're all hers. That's what Dominique and I have, and I want you to have that too."

It was nice to know that Miles only wanted to see Endz happy with the right woman. He was touched. "We'll see."

Miles turned to End and said. "We definitely will."

Jamila

Chapter 25

"How cute and sweet! Lexus cousin Chase calling to ask me for permission to ask Patresha out on a date," Dominique giggled with Ant and Dana while they walked towards the Barnes and Noble bookstore for the book signing.

Chase looked like he was deeply in love with Patresha. The way he presented himself and showed respect won Dominique over. Even by the description, she gave Miles he even respected Chase. He kind of laughed a little bit about the Chase still being a virgin part but he alright with him.

"This guy sounds like a keeper," Dana said.

"Yep!" Dominique agreed and started listing his attributes. "He's handsome. Hardworking. Has his shit together. He's a virgin."

"He's a what?" Ant stopped dead in her tracks when she heard Dominique mention the V-word to describe a young man.

"You heard me right," Dominique pulled out her phone and scrolled through her photos. She showed them a picture of Patresha and Chase arm in arm like a couple in loving bliss. "Here's a picture of them."

"Awe, they look so cute." Dana smiled. "How old is this guy?" Dana asked.

"He'll be twenty-three in about two days," Dominique answered.

"An almost twenty-three-year-old nigga that fine has never touched pussy before?" Ant was in complete disbelief. *He'd be a lot sexier without those fucking dreads!* Ant couldn't stand dreads.

"That's right," Dominique said.

"Now I've seen everything," Ant said and the ladies entered the bookstore. It was a nice manageable crowd inside. They went to grab a hardcover copy of Thuy's memoir and made their purchase at the register.

"I stayed up all night reading this book," Dana said.

"I just finished it this morning," Dominique said.

"Hey, there's only two in line for an autograph." Ant pointed out and the three ladies rushed to get in line. When it was their turn, they moved up and there was Thuy. She was looking all gorgeous in her reading glasses, a black jumpsuit with black pumps with her beautiful curly hair in a side ponytail.

"Hello ladies," Thuy greeted with her down to earth charm. "Who should I make these out to?" The ladies gave Thuy their books so she could autograph them.

"Make mine to Antoinette BKA Ant."

"Alright Ant." Thuy autographed Ant's copy and gave it to her.

"I'm Dominique."

"Alright, Dominique." Thuy autographed her copy.

"I'm Dana."

Thuy autographed Dana's copy. "Here you go, ladies."

"Thanks!" the ladies exclaimed with gratitude.

"And we would like to talk to you some more," Dominique said.

"Of course," Thuy said.

"There's nobody in line now so we can sit over here and chat," Thuy said, and the ladies followed her to a table in the corner.

"I like her," Ant said to Dominique and Dana, the two nodded in agreement.

"Hello, ladies! Glad to meet you," Thuy said.

"Mrs. Kilborn, it's a pleasure," Dana said.

"Please call me Thuy. Sit! Sit!" She offered the ladies a seat.

"We have so many questions," Dominique said as everybody took their seats. "First of all, you are an amazing woman. You are the walking definition of a real boss chick."

"Thanks. I got it from my momma," Thuy boasted.

"In your book, you mentioned how close you and your momma are," Dana said.

"That's my ride or die." Thuy nodded her head and smiles. "We've been through a lot together."

"What made you decide to write your memoir?" Ant asked.

"My favorite movie of all time is *Mommie Dearest*. I love that movie because I've always admired people who were brave enough to share their stories. With encouragement from my best friends, one of them being my personal therapist and marriage counselor, and my husband, I decided to go for it," Thuy explained.

"You and Macal still go to marriage counseling?" Dana asked.

"Hell to the yeah! Marriage is hard as fuck!" They all chuckled, but they knew Thuy was serious. "Yes, we put the past behind us, and our marriage is solid. We go to counseling to keep our marriage solid."

"I really felt that line in your book. In order to save our marriage, we had to save ourselves," Dominique pointed out.

"Exactly. We were very fucked up." Thuy had no shame in sharing her truth and the ladies admired that. "Y'all gonna check Macal's memoir? It drops next month."

"We will," Ant answered for everybody.

"What's it called again?" Dana asked.

"*A Broken Man's Redemption: Confessions of a Sex Addict,*" Thuy answered.

"Oh, he's gonna put it all out there huh?" Ant could only imagine all the sex Macal gonna say he had in his memoir. From those sex senses in Thuy's book, she had to change her panties at least three times.

"Yes, he is." Thuy knew Macal's memoir is gonna be crazy as fuck. She should know. She lived through that shit.

"What made him decide to write this memoir?" Dana asked.

"Macal wanted to show that it's never too late to try to be a better person. Also, we made a deal. If I wrote my memoir, he had to write his too," Thuy said.

"Great deal," Dominique said.

"I read the sneak peek that was at the end of your book. That was fucked up how his sex addiction got triggered." Ant shuttered at the thought of a thirteen-year-old boy getting turned on by watching his daddy and his side piece fuck. That poor

153

baby was confused. So, confused that he wanted to fuck his daddy's hoe.

"Very disturbing." Dana thought that was some sick shit.

"Yes, it was," Thuy said. "You can imagine how shocked I was when he first told me. Fallon is working on her memoir too. She wants to use her story to address the importance of getting help for mental illness. A portion of the royalties from her memoir will go to her foundation."

"That's a wonderful thing to do." Dana admired. "We'll check that out too."

"You ladies are amazing," Thuy said. Of course, she knows due to legal reasons some things in Fallon's memoir had to be omitted.

"Alright, let me get this straight," Dominique needed to get to the bottom of this other shit that was on her mind ever since she read the memoir. "I'm still blown by you and Fallon finding out y'all were sisters. It's crazy that you married her ex-husband and didn't know it at all."

"Yes! Yes!" *This world is too fucking small!* Thuy thought. "Things like that happen when your sperm donor thinks it cool to spread his community dick around."

"Girl don't I know it," Ant emphasized.

"Same here." Dana shared her empathy.

"It wouldn't surprise me. I never met the nigga," Dominique responded with a shoulder shrug and then addressed another point in the memoir. "Thuy, I can't believe your stepmother set you up like that and your daddy knew about it and said nothing. He didn't even try to stop her."

Thuy shook her head and sighed. "Unfortunately, yes."

"All that hatred because of something you had no control over." Dana was very disgusted. Who in the fuck sets up an innocent teenage girl to get raped?

"Yeah, some people are so angry and bitter to the point that they don't see the real picture," Thuy addressed.

"Tell me about it. I know what that's like," Ant said.

"You do?" Thuy asked.

154

"Yep. I'm an outside kid too," Ant confessed.

"You are?" Dominique asked.

"I thought your parents were married and then got divorced." Dana was confused.

Ant went ahead and explained the fucked-up way she was conceived. "That's true. You see, when my parents met, my daddy was already married with a family. The difference between me and Thuy here is that for one, my momma actually knew my daddy was married. However, my daddy actually did leave his first wife for my momma."

"Unbelievable," Thuy said.

"Yep," Ant said. "According to my mom, I'm the only child. According to my daddy, I'm four out of five and the youngest girl. His oldest son that he had before he met his first wife, we're cool. Then he had a set of fraternal twins, a boy and girl with his first wife. They hate my guts. I came into the picture after those two. When I was three, daddy divorced his first wife and married my mom. After my parents divorced, he married a third time and they had a boy. That's my little buddy right there! Of course, his third marriage failed too and he just got out of his sixth marriage. My daddy is a hoe, but he made sure we were all straight. I just hope he doesn't get married again. Some niggas have no business being married and my daddy is one of them. I love him, but it's the truth."

"I'd rather my daddy to just be a hoe like yours," Dana said to Ant. She then turned to Dominique and added. "Hell, I'd rather have a deadbeat daddy like yours who ran off and never came back than the motherfucker I got. Let me give you an idea of how bad my father was." She turned to Thuy and said, "Your father would be named Father of the Year compared to mine."

Thuy was on pause. "Shit that's saying something!"

"Til this day my daddy is trying to get back with my momma and she's like fuck no!" Ant chucked at her crazy ass parents. "My momma is not the typical mother. She's crazy as hell, but I wouldn't trade her for anything in the world."

"I miss my momma so much. I'll never forgive my dad for

taking her away from me," Dana said with sadness. She thought about Dominique's relationship with her mother and asked her. "Would you consider talking things out with..."

"No!" Dominique knew what Dana was suggesting and she wasn't with that shit. "I never wanna see that bitch again as long as I live!"

"I know one thing." Dana rubbed her pregnant belly. "This little girl is gonna have the best mother in the world. I can't wait to meet her."

"Congratulations!" Thuy cheered. "I hope you and your daughter have a beautiful relationship."

"Thank you." Dana's phone started to ring. She looked at the caller ID and said. "It's my fiancé. "Excuse me." She walked off to answer the call.

"There's a line forming," Thuy said. "I gotta get back."

"Okay." Ant said with understanding.

Dominique took this time to privately address something to Ant. "Glad we're alone so we can talk."

"What do you want to talk about?" Ant could tell whatever the subject was gonna be it's been heavy on Dominique's mind for some time and it had something to do with her baby sister-in-law.

"What do you think of Neil?"

"I don't like the nigga." Ant was very blunt.

"Why not?" Dominique asked.

"I don't know what the fuck is going on, but something about him rubs me the wrong way," Ant expressed her concerns.

"I felt the same way about him the first day I met him."

"You did?" Dominique nodded her head. "How about this nigga was engaged before?" Ant shared.

"He was?" This was news to Dominique.

"Yes, but the wedding was called off. The woman left him at the altar."

"Why?"

"I don't know, but Dana said after that he met her and asked her out on a date not even a full week later," Ant said.

156

"Are you serious?" Dominique shared Ant's suspicions.

"Yes. I told Dana he was moving on too fast, but her head was in the clouds to clearly think about this." Ant was really worried about Dana. "Another thing on her birthday I surprised her with a trip to Barbados."

"Ooooh, Barbados!" Dominique was impressed. "Girl you know how to do it big!"

"Well, I am my mother's daughter." Ant giggled a little bit and then got back on subject. "It was me, Dana, momma, my daddy's third wife and my oldest brother's wife on the trip. We were all having a great time and everything, but Neil was calling her too much."

Dominique raised her eyebrow. "Exactly how much was too much?"

"His ass called her at least fifty times our first day there and that went on throughout the whole trip. Keep in mind they weren't even engaged yet. Just boyfriend and girlfriend."

"What the fuck? Miles don't even call me like that when I travel alone and he's actually my damn husband!"

"I know right," Ant agreed. "Eli was cool when I went out and traveled alone. In fact, he encouraged it. And another thing before she started living with Endz Dana changed. Something about her was off and I think it had something to do with Neil."

"I wish she could get with Endz," Dominique said.

"You noticed it too?" Ant asked with amazement and glad that Dominique was as observant as she was.

"Yes. They want each other and they don't even know it."

"Well, we'll see what happens."

****

"I miss you, baby," Neil said to Dana over the phone.

"I miss you too," Dana said.

"Are you having a good day?"

"Yes, baby. How about you?"

"Not so good." Neil sighed. "I've been working like a dog.

In fact, I gotta work late again. When you coming back?"

"In about four days," Dana answered. "I'll call you when I get back home."

"Okay, baby. I love you."

"I love you too."

After the call ended, Neil kept on driving behind Chase's vehicle with him and Patresha inside. "You fat, backstabbing, stank ass hoe!" he screamed with intense hatred as he continued his stalking in Miami.

Chapter 26

Neil wasn't gonna sit around and let Patresha disrespect him like that and think she could just drop him like he wasn't shit. Oh, hell to the motherfucking no! And now her ass is all up on some simp ass nigga. They ain't done until Neil says they're done.

"I knew that hoe was scandalous!" Neil screamed at the top of his lungs as he continued to follow the couple all over town. After Patresha hung up on him, Neil had to hop on the next plane to Miami and find out where the fuck she was. He just had to remember to beat Dana back to Albany.

Chase pulled into some fancy restaurant. He parked the car and got out to open Patresha's car door for her. He gave her a quick kiss on the cheek and escorted her into the restaurant with a look on his face that said that he was the luckiest man on the planet.

Neil couldn't believe what the fuck he was witnessing. This simp dread head ass nigga is all pussy whipped over that dumb, sloppy, fat ass hoe. Driving her around in his sharp ass ride. Taking her to upscale places and dressing her up in the best designer shit like she's somebody. And if Neil didn't know any better by the way she was talking to him and carried herself around Chase, she was starting to believe it herself. That bitch ain't shit and she'll never be shit. She's only good for a private fuck and that's it. This little fool, on the other hand, was acting like he wanna wife her on the spot. Patresha was Neil's private fuck and no other nigga was gonna jack his private fuck away from him.

Neil's original plan was to wait for them to come out, but he needed to get inside to see what the fuck was going on. Besides, all this stalking was making a nigga hungry. He parked and got out of his rented candy apple red Audi SUV all decked out in his disguise. He was wearing a pair of glasses, a fake salt and pepper mustache and beard that added twenty-five years to his handsome appearance.

He walked into the restaurant and looked around for Chase

and Patresha. He spotted them sitting in a booth. As luck would have it there was an available booth right behind them.

Perfect! Neil made his way to his seat. On the way, he noticed a few sexy ass young women checking him out and smiling at him. *Maybe I should keep this look!* His ego and dick were in full force. For a man who's begging for his pregnant fiancée to move back in with him and following his former side piece who had enough of his ass Neil had a fucked-up way of thinking. Neil took his seat and listened closely to Chase and Patresha's conversation.

****

"That play was beautiful," Patresha said.

"Glad you enjoyed it," Chase said. He was looking all good with his designer navy-blue buttoned-down shirt and black slacks and black slacks with his fresh dreadlocks in a ponytail.

"How did you get those seats?" Patresha asked. "They were the perfect seats."

"One of my CNA patients has a grandson who plays for the Miami Dolphins and he hooked me up," Chase answered.

"So many surprises," Patresha said and picked at her food.

"What's wrong? You haven't touched your food. Is it bad?" Chase wanted to make sure that his lady was good and enjoying every minute of their date.

"No, it's delicious! I just don't wanna look like a pig." Patresha's body insecurities were taking over.

"Girl, you better eat that food!" Chase playfully scolded Patresha like she was a child. "Talking about you don't wanna look like a pig. This Neil nigga must've really fucked you up bad?"

"Yes, he did." Patresha sighed and continued to eat her food.

"Don't give that fuck nigga a second thought." Chase waved off the thought of Neil like his ass was irrelevant and didn't matter. "His ass is history."

"Yes, he is."

Chase started laughing. "Didn't he sound like a pathetic, weak ass, fuck nigga on the phone?"

"Yes, his punk ass did!" Patresha joined in on the laughter at Neil's expense. This was interesting. Usually, she's the butt of the jokes and being laughed at. It felt good to be on the giving end of things for a change. Especially against somebody who deserved it like Neil for example.

"Thanks for putting his bitch ass on speakerphone. I needed that laugh for the day." They kept on laughing. "What did that bitch nigga say again? Oh yeah! 'Baby, I'm sorry for everything! I've been thinking about you!'" Chase did a great Neil's fake ass begging impression.

"Shit! Maybe I should've let him beg some more before cutting his ass off mid-sentence. Then we would've had more shit to laugh at his ass about." Patresha was being petty as fuck and Chase loved it.

After a few more minutes of laughing at that clown ass nigga, Chase lifted his champagne glass and Patresha did the same. "To new beginnings."

"To new beginnings," Patresha repeated and they toasted their glasses.

As the two enjoyed their meal, Milo and Sadie approached their table. "Chase!" Milo called out.

Chase looked up and saw his parents. "Mom! Dad! How are you?"

"We're great. We're about to sit at our table." Sadie said.

Chase went ahead and made the big introduction. "Mom, Dad, this is Patresha. She's Lexus' best friend and my woman. Patresha, these are my parents, Milo and Sadie."

"Nice to meet you," Chase's parents greeted and hugged Patresha.

"So, you are the beautiful young lady who makes my son smile," Milo said.

"I'm nothing special. Just me." Patresha shyly giggled.

"You are special," Chase said to Patresha.

"He's right and don't you ever let anybody make you feel

any different," Sadie dropped an important jewel on Patresha.

"Okay." Patresha let Sadie's words sink in. "It was nice to meet y'all."

"Nice to meet you too," Milo said and then turned to his lovely wife. "Let's take our seats." He turned to their only child and his beautiful alluring date one last time before taking their leave. "See y'all later. Bye, bye."

"Bye!" Chase and Patresha waved goodbye.

"They seem very nice," Patresha said.

"They're good people." Chase nodded.

Patresha took a quick look around at her current surroundings and took a deep breath like she was breathing clean fresh air. "So, this is what it's like."

"What, what's like?"

"To be out on a date with a man. One who ain't ashamed to be seen with me in public and he actually introduced me to his parents." This was all foreign to Patresha.

Chase didn't say anything. He just sat there in silence until their waiter came back. "Sir, would you like anything else?"

"No sir we'll have the check," Chase said. The waiter gave Chase the bill. He pulled out a wad of cash and gave it to the waiter. "Here you go and keep the change."

"Thank you!" The waiter said with deep gratitude.

"Alright let's go!" Chase took Patresha by the hand.

"Where are we going?" Patresha was all giddy like a schoolgirl.

"You'll see my baby."

And so will I! Neil thought as he slammed his money down for his meal and inconspicuously followed the couple outside.

Chapter 27

"This beach is beautiful!" Patresha exclaimed with excitement. She and Chase took a stroll on Miami Beach enjoying the night air under the stars and the beautiful glowing moonlight.

"It is, isn't it?" Chase took in the romantic scenery. As they both let the beautiful ocean water splash on their bare feet while walking on the smooth sand, Chase saw a bench nearby and led the way.

When they reached the bench, Chase took a seat. He motioned for Patresha to lay across the bench to lay on his lap with his arms wrapped around her. "There we go."

"You're so sweet!" Patresha made herself comfortable in Chase's arms. "Why were you quiet during the rest of the dinner?"

"I was thinking about what you said." Chase looked into Patresha's eyes and asked. "Do you trust me?"

"Yes, Chase, I do."

"What did Neil do to you?"

Patresha sighed. She trusted Chase, but she was scared of what he would think of her. "I knew this date was going too well. You might not wanna be with me if I tell you."

"Patresha nothing you say is gonna change my mind about you," Chase assured his lady. "I wanna know about you. What happened to you? Who hurt you? I wanna know so I can understand you and make sure that you never hurt again."

He's spitting some deep ass shit! How could Patresha shy away from that? "Okay." She sighed. "Here it goes." She basically told Chase her whole life story. From her difficult childhood to her high school days to her traumatic and humiliating ordeal with Neil. "And that's my story."

Chase was breathing heavily looking like he wanted to kill somebody. "That motherfucker! He preyed on you! If I ever see that nigga on the street, I'm gonna fuck his ass up on sight!"

It took a while for Chase to calm down. He looked into Patresha's beautiful eyes. "Patresha, I know we haven't known each other long, but I can't help how I feel about you. I love you, baby girl!"

"Chase! I love you too!" Patresha said.

Chase pulled Patresha into a deep, passionate, and romantic kiss. It was strong and electrifying. This was the best feeling Patresha has ever felt in her life. She didn't want this magical moment to end.

When the kiss broke, Patresha was the first to speak. "Can I ask you something?"

"Sure, anything beautiful."

"How are you a fine and sexy ass virgin at almost twenty-three?" Patresha had to get to the bottom of this.

Chase chuckled because he was expecting this question sooner or later. "Well, it's kind of by choice, but not really. When I was in high school, my first girlfriend and I broke up before the relationship got that far. My high school sweetheart moved away before our senior year. While we were together, she wasn't ready, and I respected that. Since then I mostly went to class, worked, and kept busy. I didn't really give myself the time to date like that let alone have sex."

"So, you were basically more focused on working on you?"

"Right."

"Also, Lexus really helped me look at sex and intimacy in different ways. I worked on using my best judgment and I helped her do the same. I'll know when the time is right and with the woman's consent of course," Chase said.

"Why can't more men be like you?" Patresha was super impressed with Chase's maturity and the way he thinks and handles his business.

"I honestly don't know." Chase shrugged his shoulders. "Ms. Glover?"

"Yes, Mr. Roberts."

"May I kiss you again?"

"Yes, you may."

The couple started another hot and passionate make-out session. Out of nowhere, Patresha broke the kiss. "What's wrong baby?" Chase asked with concern.

"I'm not sure but I have this weird feeling that we're being watched." Patresha looked around slightly frantic.

"Who would be watching us?" Chase looked around himself. "I don't think anybody is watching us, but if it'll make you feel better, we'll walk down to the end of the beach to check out the action. What do you think?"

Patresha looked over where Chase was pointing and saw a lot of lights flashing and it looked like the area was popping with a lot of entertainment. "Before I answer that. Are you tired?"

"Nope. You?"

"Nope."

"Alright let's go."

Chase and Patresha helped each other get off the bench and started to walk towards the lighted area to check out the beach's nightlife and mingle with the crowd.

Out of nowhere, Neil emerged from behind the palm trees that were behind the bench Chase and Patresha were sitting seething like a motherfucker. Listening to Patresha's pathetic ass sob story was making him fucking sick. He was struggling to keep his dinner down. What made Neil sicker was Chase pussy ass was actually listening like he gave a fuck.

Weak ass nigga! Neil thought. "His ass is probably a faggot anyway!" He scoffed. "Why else would his ass be cool with never getting pussy? Talking all that shit about fucking me up! Nigga please!"

Neil went on with his private tirade. He was heated. Not only did Patresha think she could just dismiss him like he was nothing, but she was all up on the first nigga that gave her the time of day. That part didn't surprise Neil because that's how he got her fat hoe ass in the first place. With her ass telling that fool all their business, had him incensed.

However, all of that shit was not what fucked with Neil the most. He could deal with hearing Patresha's woe as me whining. He always let that shit go out one ear and out the other anyway. Hell, even dismissing him, getting with another nigga, and telling all their business wasn't the worst of that. In fact, none of that shit surprised Neil.

What fucked him up the most was that Patresha humiliated him. The bitch put him on speakerphone so she could clown him with that virgin nigga. The nerve of that stank ass hoe! Having that nigga mock him!

"Didn't he sound like a pathetic weak ass fuck nigga on the phone? Yes, his punk ass did! Thanks for putting his bitch ass on speakerphone. I needed that laugh for the day. What did that bitch nigga say again? Oh yeah! 'Baby I'm sorry for everything! I've been thinking about you!' Shit! Maybe I should've let him beg some more before cutting his ass off mid-sentence. Then we would've had more shit to laugh at his ass about."

"Aaaaaah!" Neil screamed as he replayed Patresha and Chase's mocking in his head. "No bitch makes a fool out of Neil Carlos Henderson and gets away with that shit!" He didn't know how, he didn't know how long it was gonna take him and he didn't know when, but he was gonna put Patresha back in her place once and for all.

Chapter 28

"Happy Birthday dear Chase! Happy birthday to you!" Aiesha sang beautifully as Chase blew out all twenty-three candles of his birthday cake. Everyone was gathered at Milo and Sadie's house sitting around the dining room table enjoying their only child's birthday dinner. The birthday cake was beautifully decorated in black and gray frosting with the words Happy Twenty-Third Birthday Chase written in cursive with his likeness dressed in a black suit with his jacket opened up like Superman exposing his gray scrubs.

"That was beautiful, baby," Bryce complimented his wife's beautiful singing as she took her seat next to him.

"Thank baby." Aiesha blushed.

"Aiesha, girl, I felt that!" Chase rubbed his chest where his heart laid. "Thanks, cuz. Momma, thanks for dinner. You hooked it up!"

"Anything for my baby," Sadie said. The birthday dinner she cooked was like a Thanksgiving feast. There was macaroni and cheese, hen, collard greens, chicken dressing, fried chicken, the works.

"Let's not forget about this delicious birthday cake," Lexus said as she stuffed her face. "Aunt Sadie, this is off the chain!"

"Thanks, but I can't take all the credit. Your Uncle Milo helped me out." Sadie rubbed her husband's back.

"Dad when did you start baking?" Chase asked. He never knew Milo would ever be into baking.

"Boy, there's a lot about me you don't know." Milo chuckled. "Your grandma and granddaddy made sure me, and your Aunt Colleen knew how to cook, clean, take care of the house, and was on top of our schoolwork."

"Momma made sure we were both in that kitchen when she was cooking." Bryce pointed at himself and Lexus.

"Let's not forget about her cleaning and homework schedules," Lexus said. She turned to her father who had sadness in his eyes. 'Til this day, August still grieved over his wife's murder. "I'm sorry, daddy."

"It's okay, baby girl," August assured his concerned daughter. "Your mother's spirit is in all of us. Cal was an amazing woman."

"I always wondered, Uncle August. Why did you call Aunt Colleen, Cal?" Chase asked.

August chuckled before explaining his pet name for Colleen. "Cal is short for calculator. Not only was Cal the most beautiful girl in school, but she was also almost the smartest. She was our class valedictorian. Graduated from college with honors. A beauty with numbers." He grabbed Lexus' hand and looked into her eyes. "You remind me so much of your mother. You have her intelligence and her beauty." He then looked over at his son. "When I see how dedicated you are to your marriage and building your home that's so much like your mother. She took commitments seriously just like you."

"You wanna open your presents?" Patresha asked Chase.

"Yes, baby." Chase smiled.

"They're on the couch in the living room," Wyatt said.

Chase rushed over to the living room couch like he was a little kid on Christmas morning, and everybody followed and gathered around him. They all stood silently as Chase opened his presents. His grandparents gave him a pair of black Stacy Adams shoes. Bryce and Aiesha gave him a Miami Dolphins blanket. Lexus and Wyatt gave him the brand-new NFL Madden game. August gave him a Platinum iPhone case. His parents already had his new condo decorated and furnished.

"Here's my present." Patresha handed Chase her present.

"Let me see what my baby girl gave me." Chase opened the present to see what was inside. It was a wooden box.

"Turn the wheel," Patresha insisted with excitement with a big smile on her face.

"Okay." Chase turned the wheel around and around until something popped out. It was a jack-in-a-box holding a picture of Patresha and Chase at the beach carnival. Everybody laughed. Chase pulled Patresha into a kiss. "This is great. Thank you, baby."

"Happy birthday Chase! Sorry, I couldn't find a clown suit," Patresha joked.

"Clown suit?" Aiesha was clueless.

"Inside joke," Chase said and turned his attention back to his woman. "Thank you, baby, for making this the best birthday of my life."

"Anytime Chase." Patresha smiled.

"This is so beautiful," August observed Chase and Patresha's loving interaction. "Young love." He pulled Lexus and Patresha into a big hug and kissed their foreheads. "I'm so glad to see both my girls with good respectable young men who always show them love and utmost respect."

Patresha looked at August. "You think of me as your girl?"

"Girl, you know you're one of my kids too." August laughed, giving Patresha another hug and kiss on the cheek to prove his point.

That really touched Patresha. She always wanted a father who loved her. The last time she saw her biological father, she was six years old and he walked past her like he didn't even see her. He was with his newly pregnant wife who was the woman he left her mother for. That memory really fucked with her. She hugged August and said. "Thanks, Mr. Phillips."

"You a sweet girl, Patresha. You deserve a good and happy life."

"Uncle August is right, baby," Chase said and took Patresha by the hand.

"Hey, it's still your birthday! Why don't you kids make the most of it?" Milo suggested.

"Are you sure dad?" Chase asked.

"Yeah go out! Live a little!" August encouraged.

"Alright if you insist," Chase said and he and Patresha were arm and arm ready to head out.

"Bryce, Aiesha, are y'all gonna join us?" Lexus asked with Wyatt's arms wrapped around her.

"We'd love to, but I got some schoolwork to catch up on

after we clean up here." Aiesha was taking online classes for her master's degree.

"Baby, you don't have to worry about cleaning up here. You go ahead home and study," Bryce said to Aiesha.

"Okay, I'll see you at home after you finish up here." Aiesha kissed Bryce. "Bye baby and you kids have fun and be safe," she said as she followed the two young couples out the door.

"We will!" Chase, Patresha, Lexus, and Wyatt said simultaneously.

******

I Am da Club by Plies was playing at Gold Five. The club was jumping with everybody dancing and having a good time.

"Happy Birthday baby!" Patresha was all up on Chase in the VIP section.

"Thanks, baby." Chase grabbed a handful of Patresha's ass and planted a deep kiss on her. "Hey, let's take a picture!" He took his phone out and snapped a few selfies with his woman. "I'm about to post these on Facebook right now."

"Let's get some more pictures of the happy couple." Wyatt took his phone out and started taking some pictures of Chase and Patresha. They also took some more pictures of each other. Wyatt and Lexus loved the deep affection Chase and Patresha had for each other. They were enjoying each other like they didn't have a care in the world.

"I love you, baby!" Patresha smiled and kissed Chase.

"I love you too, baby!" Chase flashed his sexy ass grin and returned the kiss.

"I gotta go to the bathroom. I'll be right back." Patresha gave Chase a final kiss before she left.

"I'll be waiting right here for you, baby." Chase smiled.

Patresha found the bathroom to take care of her business. Afterwards, she washed her hands and checked herself out in the mirror. When she got out of the bathroom, she felt a massive amount of heat hit her all at once. "Shit I'm hot!"

170

To her right, Patresha saw the opened doors to the deck outside and decided to take a breather. When she stepped outside, she embraced the cool air and took a seat at a vacant table across from two ladies that were talking amongst themselves.

"This feels so much better." Patresha dug into her purse to pull out her phone. "Let me call Chase so he can join me out here."

"Excuse me, miss!" Patresha looked up and saw an older man wearing a pair of glasses and had a salt and pepper mustache and beard rubbing his knee.

Patresha knew he was talking to her because she was closer to him and the two ladies were too far to even hear him. "Yes sir?"

"My knee is bothering me a little bit. I forgot to take my arthritis medication and I am having trouble getting to my car. Can you help me?" The older man pleaded.

"Of course!" Patresha rushed over to the older man's aide. She let him put his arm across the back of her shoulders and she proceeded to help him walk to his car.

"Thank you so much, sweetheart!" The older man was deeply grateful.

"It's okay. I got you," Patresha assured him. The parking lot was not a long walk. "Where's your car?"

"It's over there." The older man pointed to a candy apple red Audi SUV.

Patresha led him to his vehicle and made sure he was able to get his keys and helped him open the door and helped him in the driver's seat. "You got it?" Patresha asked.

"Yes, I got it. How can I ever repay you?"

"Oh, don't worry about it. Just being a Good Samaritan."

"Oh, but I insist, Patresha."

"It's okay I'm good! Goodnight and be careful." Patresha turned around to walk away. It took her a good five seconds to realize something was off. *Did he just say my name?*

BOOM!

Jamila

Patresha's thought was cut short by a blow to the head.

Chapter 29

"What's taking her so long to come out?" Chase was impatiently waiting for Patresha to come back.

"I don't know." Lexus shrugged her shoulders. "Do you think she's sick?"

"I don't think so," Chase said. "She was just fine before she went into the bathroom."

"I'll check on her real quick to be sure." Lexus offered.

"Thanks, cuz," Chase said with gratitude.

Lexus was about to head for the bathroom, but she stopped when she got a text notification. She pulled out her phone and saw a text message from Patresha. "Oh, she just texted me."

"What did she say?" Wyatt asked.

Lexus began to read Patresha's text message aloud:

Patresha: *I'm sorry for the way I left. I didn't feel well so I took an Uber back to the house.*

Lexus: *That's okay. I can come over to sit with you. Chase is worried about you.*

Patresha: *No, you don't have to go through all of that trouble. I'm about to go to sleep anyway. Goodnight!*

"I guess we'll see her tomorrow," Lexus said. "She said she was going to bed."

"Alright," Chase said with relief. "At least she's safe and sound at the house."

"Exactly!" Wyatt agreed. "Patresha is asleep and Aiesha is at the house, right?" Chase and Lexus nodded their heads in agreement. "So, if Patresha needs something, Aiesha will be right there to take care of her."

"You're right," Chase said. "Patresha will feel better after a good night's sleep. After all, what could happen to her?"

******

173

Jamila

"Wake up bitch!" A firm slap to the side of her face woke
Patresha up. When her eyes adjusted to the light, she found
herself in a room on a bed with her wrists tied behind her back
and she was completely naked.

"Where am I?" Patresha whimpered. "What the fuck is going
on? He..."

Whap!

"Scream again and you're a dead fat hoe!"

This time Patresha was able to see who her sick ass kidnap-
per was. "Neil? What are you doing here?" Patresha thought she
saw the last of this psycho nigga. It was easy to figure out the
older man was Neil in disguise, and he lured her away to knock
her out and kidnap her.

"I was trying to make up with you, but your ungrateful ass
was too busy fucking around on me!"

This nigga is crazy! Patresha knew Neil was a sick abusive
manipulative fuck but she had no idea it was to this extreme. "I
told you it was over! We're done! What you did to me..."

"I was about to apologize to you!" Neil interrupted with his
fake pleas.

"Bullshit!" Patresha snapped. She had enough of Neil's sick
ass games. "I've moved on and I suggest you do the same." On
second thought. Neil didn't need to move on. This nigga needs to
be stopped before he fuck up another woman's life.

Neil grabbed Patresha's face and squeezed tightly. "Who the
fuck do you think you are? Telling me what the fuck to do!" He
hissed with poisonous venom in her face. "Your fat ass acting all
brand new because of that dread head ass nigga. You think
you're so motherfucking special. Guess what bitch? Your nasty
fat ass ain't shit and will never be shit!" He let go of his grip on
her face with hate and disgust.

"You've been stalking us." Patresha was terrified.

"Ever since you hung up on me and had that simp ass virgin
nigga laughing at me!" Neil confessed with the demeanor of
somebody who wanted to tear shit up.

Patresha's eyes bugged out in horror. "You really were

174

watching us at the beach and dinner!"

Neil flashed a huge evil grin like the Joker from *Batman.* "Bingo!"

"Please, Neil! Don't hurt me!" Deep down Patresha knew begging and pleading for her life was futile, but begging and pleading was all she could do at this point. "Just let me go and I won't say anything! I won't call the police! I won't tell Miss Dana! You'll never hear from me again. Just please let me go!"

"Oh, I'll let you go." Neil had a black bag that was placed in a chair. He walked over to the bag to open it and pulled out a ball gag. He put his disguise back on and walked back over to Patresha. "I will let you go, but first..." He put the ball gag on her. "You need to be reminded who the fuck you crossed and what the fuck you really are!"

"Neil! Don't do it please!" Patresha cried out through the ball gag as Neil began to undress.

Jamila

Chapter 30

"I win again!" Wyatt cheered when we won another game of pool in the recreation room of Gold Five.

"Shit nigga! You killing me!" Chase dug in his pocket and gave Wyatt fifty dollars.

"Hey, don't hate the playa, hate the game!" Wyatt boasted and put his winnings in his pocket.

"Thank you so much for that 1990s reference," Chase dryly commented.

"And don't forget my good luck charm right here." Wyatt pulled Lexus in his arms and planted a big fat kiss on her.

"Congratulations baby!" Lexus smiled.

"So, Lexus, you just gonna do your blood like that huh?" Chase playfully sounded betrayed with his arms out.

"Chase quit being a sore loser." Lexus laughed and walked over to hug her big cousin. "You know I got love for you."

"Let me go to the bathroom. I'll be right back," Lexus said.

"Hurry back baby!" Wyatt shouted out.

"Alright," Lexus said and went to the bathroom. She found an available stall to take care of her business.

While Lexus was in the bathroom, she heard two toilets flush. Two women walked out of the stalls and went to the sinks to wash their hands. "I had a good time. Thanks for the night out," the first woman said.

"Anytime," the second woman said. "You needed to get out. It's been two months and you need to quit moping over that nothing ass fuck nigga."

"You're right, girl! Fuck him!"

"That's the spirit!" The ladies laughed.

"You see how fast that old ass nigga ran across the street?"

"Are you talking about that dude that girl was helping get to his car? I think he was wearing a navy-blue shirt and a pair of black slacks?" the first woman asked.

"That's the dude!" the second woman confirmed. "I don't know why his ass needed help. The way he ran across that street earlier. Now that I think about it, he wasn't built like an old man. It was like his face said he was in his fifties, but his body said he was at least mid-twenties."

"Well, you know how some of these old niggas are these days. Working out every day to stay in shape to keep up with young pussy." The first woman chuckled.

"You right about that," the second woman agreed, and the ladies left.

Lexus exited the stall after the ladies left and washed her hands. Actually, she'd been finished using the bathroom, but she was being nosy. Normally, she wasn't nosy like that, but there was something about the ladies' conversation that caught her attention for some reason.

After washing her hands and checking herself out in the mirror, Lexus went back to join her man and cousin at the pool table. "I'm back!" Lexus made her presence known and took her place next to Wyatt.

"Shit!" Chase barely missed the last shot. "I almost had it!"

It was Wyatt's turn and he made the shot. "I win again!"

"Lexus, you a fucking jinx! I was doing great until your ass came back!" Chase glared at her and gave Wyatt another fifty dollars.

"Boy hush!" Lexus waved off Chase and then turned to Wyatt. "You know I'm gonna go back to the house. I'll check up on Patresha to see if she's feeling better."

"I appreciate that," Chase said.

"Of course." Lexus pulled her phone out to make a call. "I'll call Aiesha to see if she can pick me up."

"Hello," Aiesha answered the phone.

"Aiesha, can you pick me up?" Lexus asked. "I'm a little tired and Wyatt and Chase are playing pool trying to hustle each other." All of the sudden she switched to a whisper. "Actually, Wyatt is doing all the hustling."

"I hear that shit!" Chase objected as Wyatt set up the balls for the next game.

"Those niggas better be lucky me and Bryce ain't playing.

We would've cleaned both they asses out!" Aiesha bragged and she and Lexus laughed.

"What's so funny?" Chase asked.

"Aiesha said if she and Bryce were playing, they would've cleaned both y'all asses out!" Lexus repeated her sister-in-law's words.

"Whatever!" Wyatt blew that comment off.

"Uh...Wyatt. Bryce and Aiesha are beasts in pool," Chase confirmed.

"I'd like to see that shit!" Wyatt chuckled.

"Alright Lexus just tell me where you are, and I'll be right there," Aiesha said. "I'm already in the car driving as we speak."

"We're at Gold Five and I also wanted to check on Patresha. She went back to the house earlier because she wasn't feeling well," Lexus said.

"Wow! I must've been working on my schoolwork super hard in the office because I didn't hear her come in." Aiesha shook her head.

"You didn't?" Lexus was baffled.

"No, I didn't. Maybe I had the TV up too loud." Aiesha said.

"Alright I'm gonna be outside so you can see me when you pull up," Lexus said.

"Okay. I'll be there in about seven minutes."

"Alright." Lexus hung up and hugged and kissed Wyatt. "I'm about to go. Bye baby."

"Bye baby," Wyatt said.

Lexus walked over to hug Chase and kissed him on the forehead. "Bye Chase."

"Bye, little cuz. Now that you're leaving maybe I can win some of my money back," Chase joked.

Lexus yanked Chase's dreads that were in a ponytail. "Nigga, I ain't fucking with you." And she headed out to wait for her ride.

******

"Thanks for the makeup fuck!" Neil pushed Patresha's sexually violated body out of his rented vehicle in front of Bryce and Aiesha's house and drove off.

Patresha struggled to get off the ground and walked towards the front door in a daze. She was hoping that humiliating ordeal was a dream, but it wasn't It was a living breathing nightmare. Neil tore apart all of her holes. Vaginal, anal, and mouth. She got her key out and let herself inside the house.

No one was home. Patresha rushed into her guestroom and shut the door. She ran into the bathroom and ran her a bubble bath. She got undressed and looked in the mirror. She thought it was over. She thought she was gonna start a whole new life filled with love and happiness with Chase, but it was now over. Neil made sure of that. Patresha turned the water off and sat in the tub. She started to scrub away all traces of Neil off her body.

Knock! Knock!

"Patresha!" Lexus called out.

"I'm in the bathroom, soaking in the tub!" Patresha screamed out.

"I wanted to check to see if you were feeling better," Lexus said.

"Yes, I'm feeling better. I'm not at one hundred percent but I'll get there." Patresha struggled to lie through her teeth.

"That's good," Lexus said. "Chase was very worried about you. We all were."

Hearing Chase's name being mentioned made Patresha burst into tears. "Can you tell him that I'm okay and that I'll talk to him tomorrow?"

"I will. Goodnight."

"Goodnight."

Patresha covered her face and whispered to herself weakly. "I'll never be okay! I'll never be okay!"

Chapter 31

Ant and her two precious children were sitting in the visiting room of the Dekalb County Correctional Facility waiting patiently for the inmate they were there to see come out. Ant pulled out her phone to check her business page on Facebook for reviews and what needs to be updated.

"Granddaddy!" Connie and EJ cheered and ran up to the older, bald, gray, bearded version of their deceased father.

"Hey, kids!" Lando in his orange jumpsuit hugged his grandchildren. "How y'all doing?"

"We're doing great!" Connie answered.

"How's school going?" Lando asked and he and his grand-kids took a seat at an empty table.

"It's great. We went on a field trip," EJ answered.

"I'm learning a new song to play on the piano," Connie said.

After checking her social media accounts, Ant walked over to the table. "Hey kids, I need to talk to your granddaddy. Y'all know the drill."

"Yes, momma!" Connie said as she took EJ by the hand and the two went over to the play area where the other kids who were visiting their loved ones were playing.

"Hey, Lando." Ant greeted her father-in-law with a hug.

"Hello, Antionette."

Throughout her whole marriage to Eli, the main argument they had was bringing their children to see Lando. Eli hated his father for what he did to his beautiful and beloved mother and stepfather. That nigga fucked up his own family and as far as Eli was concerned, his abusive ass didn't deserve a relationship with his grandchildren.

However, Ant saw things differently. What Lando did was terrible, but she also saw this as a learning experience for Lando and the children. Lando needed to be reminded of what he threw away and the kids needed to know where they can end up if they make bad fucked up decisions. Eli gave in when EJ turned three years old.

"How you holding up in here?" Ant asked.

"I'm maintaining." Lando sighed. "How's Dana?"

"She's good." Ant nodded.

"She can't wait to have her baby girl. She just left this morning." Ant said.

"Did you ask her?"

"Yes, I did, and her answer is still the same."

"Shit!" Lando huffed with disappointment.

"You didn't think that she was gonna come see you, did you?" Ant wanted Lando to be realistic. "What you put her through and what you did to end up here was pretty fucked up."

"I know Antionette and I'm sorry. I wish she could forgive me. I wanna see her. Can you help me with that? Please!" Lando pleaded.

"That's not up to me. That's up to Dana. All I can do is pass the message along." Ant shrugged her shoulders.

"That's all I ask," Lando said. "My son chose well. You were an amazing wife and a wonderful mother to my grandbabies. I really appreciate you letting me see them. Why do you do it?"

"I do it mostly for them." Ant motioned her head towards her children who were playing with another boy and girl in the play area. "They need to know what happens to people who make fucked up choices."

"Right." Lando sadly agreed. "Shit, I fucked up!" He wouldn't let himself cry because he knew his tears were pointless. He was filled with deep regret.

"I'm sorry." Ant grabbed Lando's hand. She could tell this was a remorseful broken man.

"No, don't be. I brought this shit on myself." Lando accepted his fate long ago.

Another reason Ant still visits Lando is because he is actually taking full responsibility for his actions. He's not one of these bitter inmates who refuses to take accountability, being pissed and resentful because they got caught. Lando was at least man enough to admit that he deserves to be locked up for the rest of his life.

"Maybe someday Dana will forgive you and want to see you again," Ant said with hope.

Lando decided to change the subject. "What do you think of Dana's fiancé?

"She could do better," Ant answered bluntly.

"She deserves the best."

"Yes, she does."

"Antionette, as an old nigga who completely fucked up big time, please do me the biggest favor of my life." Ant remained silent and listened to Lando's request. "Make sure my baby girl and my grandbabies are living a wonderful life. Promise me that they are happy and healthy."

"Of course, I will Lando."

"Good. Also, I really wanna stress this with my whole body and soul."

"What's that?"

Lando looked dead into Ant's eyes and said the realest shit ever. "Make sure Dana does not end up with a man like me!"

Jamila

Chapter 32

"Welcome home baby!" Neil kissed Dana as he grabbed her last bag and entered the house. "I missed you so much."

"It feels so good to be home! I missed you too!" Dana was all smiles.

"And I promise you will not regret moving back home." Neil sounded very sincere. "Baby, I'm sorry for everything I put you through. I'm a changed man. I love you and I want you to be my wife."

"I love you too, Neil." Dana took a seat on the couch to rest. "I want us to start over and the first step is planning our wedding. Let's set a date!"

"I couldn't agree more." Neil joined Dana on the couch. "When is a good date?"

"I think after our baby girl is born so I can get my body right for the dress." Dana chuckled and rubbed her pregnant belly.

"Girl, you know you sexy as fuck." Neil pulled Dana into his arms.

"Do you really think so?" Dana blushed.

"Yes, baby girl." Neil kissed Dana. "And I can't wait to meet my beautiful little girl!" He gave Dana's belly a rub.

"Those presents Ant gave me are a great start for the nursery." Dana looked over at the corner at the presents.

"Yeah. We need to figure out what room are we gonna use for the nursery," Neil said.

"We'll figure out something." Dana sighed and rubbed her lower back with both hands.

Neil looked over at the slightly uncomfortable look on Dana's face. "What's wrong, baby?"

"My back is hurting a bit." Dana groaned in pain.

"Awe! Let me take you upstairs and I'll take care of that aching back for you," Neil offered.

"Thanks, baby!" Dana managed to crack a smile through the pain.

Neil got off the couch and lifted Dana off the couch and

carried her up the stairs and into the master bedroom. He gently laid her on her stomach on the bed. Neil undressed Dana and positioned himself behind her and used his hands to caress her back.

Neil massaged Dana's back and focused on the area that she complained about the pain. His hands felt so good on her skin. Dana loved it when he touched her like this. She felt so relaxed.

"You feel so good, baby," Neil whispered into Dana's ear. "I wanna make love to you."

"Oh, yeah baby!" Dana moaned back. "Make love to me, baby."

Neil slipped out of his clothes with a quickness. He leaned on top of Dana's back and slid his dick inside her tight and super slippery pregnant pussy. "Aaaah!" Neil moaned out. He savored the first three pumps. "I missed my pussy!" He put emphasis on the word my.

"Ooooh!" Dana busted a fat nut on Neil's dick. It felt so good. "This feels so good!"

"Does it, baby?" Neil moaned as he reached under Dana to grab her titties to give them a squeeze. He squeezed her titties as he used his dick to dig deeper inside her. "You'll never leave me again, right?"

"I'll never leave you again baby!" Dana screamed with intense pleasure as she came again.

You better not bitch!

Chapter 33

"What am I gonna do?" Patresha's eyes watered as she stared at the positive pregnancy test in her hand. She desperately tried to put what Neil did to her in Miami behind her. She almost did, but the bombshell growing in her womb gave her a reality check. She didn't tell anybody what happened. Patresha ended up being a bigger mess than she was before she went to Miami and that's exactly what Neil wanted.

All of the sudden, her phone rang. It was Neil. She never wanted to see him again, but she knew she had to talk to him. After all, he is the father of her baby. She went ahead and took the call.

"Hi, baby!"

Patresha was disgusted at the gall of this bastard to try to sweet-talk her after the humiliation he put her through.

"Neil," Patresha said with absolutely no emotion whatsoever.

"Patresha, baby girl, I'm sorry for everything I put you through." Neil went straight to playing his sick ass mind games, but Patresha was totally over it. "I also wanted to let you know that I forgive you for..."

"I'm pregnant!" Patresha didn't know how she managed to get the words out, but it just came out of nowhere.

"You are?"

"Yes, I am. I am pregnant," Patresha repeated. "You are the father. The baby was obviously conceived the night you raped me."

Hearing the 'R' word triggered something in Neil which made him drop his bullshitting act. "Bitch, nobody raped your fat ass!"

"There you go again." Patresha was done with Neil's sick ass games. "Calling me names and shit. I'm gonna tell everybody what you did to me!"

"Like anybody is gonna believe that shit!" Neil scoffed.

"I'm pregnant with your baby and I have friends who can vouch for me!" she yelled. "I also have some people on my side like Chase, my sister, and her husband."

"Oh, your friends and your simp ass virgin nigga. Your sister and her husband. You think they wanna have anything to do with you?" Neil teased.

"Why wouldn't they?"

"Patresha, do you really wanna embarrass your sister any more than you already have? Especially after everything she's done for you?" Neil subtly teased. "It doesn't surprise me because you are kind of an ungrateful hoe!"

"What the fuck are you talking about?" Patresha was getting annoyed. She was so pissed at herself for ever getting involved with this psycho nigga in any way, shape, or form.

"I just find it funny that some wholesome virgin has a fat, sloppy, nasty, stank pile of shit, porn star for his queen. What a weak simp ass nigga." Neil chuckled.

What the fuck is he talking about? Patresha thought. "What do you mean porn star?" Patresha got a text notification. It was a text message from Neil. She opened the message and it was just a link. She clicked on the link and was horrified that it was a Pornhub video featuring her and Neil. Neil's face couldn't be seen, but hers was right there for the whole world to see.

"How could you do this to me?" Patresha burst into tears.

"You did it to yourself," Neil responded without a shred of guilt.

"I hate you!" Patresha screamed with shame. "You ruined my life!"

"Oh, shut your whiny, overly dramatic ass up and live with it." Neil dismissed Patresha's heartbroken cries like they don't matter. "Nobody wants your nasty, weak hoe ass! You should be grateful any nigga wanted to stick their dick in your pussy in the first place. You right! We're done! Fuck you and that little bastard in your fat ass blubber gut!"

Neil's words were destroying Patresha inch by inch. "What am I gonna do?"

"You asking me like I give a fuck! Maybe you should kill yourself, bitch!" Neil answered with coldness in his voice to bring home his true feelings for Patresha. "That would be the smartest thing your dumb ass ever did. Have a nice life! If you don't who gives a fuck!" And just like that Neil hung up.

With the phone still to her ear, Patresha was still standing there still processing every terrible, disgusting, evil thing Neil has ever said and done to her up until this point. Patresha looked down at her phone and said, "There's only one thing I can do."

******

"You okay baby?" Darnella appeared in the doorway in the nude smiling at Neil.

"I'll feel better when I tear that pussy up!" Neil stroked his dick as he focused on Darnella's sexy ass body as she strutted over to Neil. She let him grab her and pin her down on the bed on her back with her legs wide opened. He climbed on top of her and shoved his dick deep inside her wet awaiting pussy.

"Oh, take this pussy baby!" Darnella screamed with ecstasy as Neil stretched her pussy out and letting her natural juices cover his dick by busting fat nuts. She was cumming nonstop.

While Neil was beating the pussy up, his phone started to ring. He stopped for a brief moment to grab the phone from the dresser to see who was calling him. "Fuck that bitch!" He tossed the phone back on the dresser which had Dana's picture flashing on the caller ID.

Jamila

Chapter 34

"Neil, where are you?" Dana sighed impatiently. She was cooking a romantic dinner for Neil. She wanted everything to be perfect. She took the lasagna out of the oven and placed it on top of the stove.

Her phone rang and she quickly took it out of her pocket to answer assuming it was Neil. "Hello! Where are you?"

"Baby girl! What's the fire?" Endz asked with concern.

"Oh Endz! It's just you," Dana responded with disappointment. "I thought you were Neil."

"Sorry to disappoint you." Endz played like he was offended.

"Nigga don't be acting all upset and shit!" Dana laughed. "You know I was just bullshitting!"

"And you know this man!" Endz finished Smokey's closing line in *Friday* and the two busted out laughing like crazy.

"So, what's up?"

"You remember that question you asked me?"

"What question?"

"I know you meant to ask Neil, but technically you asked me where I was," Endz said.

"Okay, so, where are you?" Dana went along with it.

"Come outside," Endz instructed Dana.

Dana opened the front door and stepped outside. She saw Endz leaning on the side of a brand-new midnight-blue Rolls Royce. It was the most beautiful car she has ever seen in her life. "Oh shit!" She rushed over to the car.

"Whoa!" Dana peaked inside and admired the black and twenty-four karat gold interior. "This car is beautiful!"

"Thank you! Thank you!" Endz smiled with pride at his new toy. "I just picked it up." He looked over at Dana and noticed how in awe of his new ride. "Do you like the car?"

"I love the car!" Dana was cheesing her ass off. Her smile captivated Endz. Her smile made her even more beautiful than she already was.

"You really love this car."

"Yes, I do."

Endz took her hand and rubbed it. "Would you like to take a ride with me?"

"Me? Ride in the car with you?" Dana wanted to make sure that she heard Endz right.

"Yeah, girl!"

"Of course!" Dana answered without even thinking it over. She was in love with that car. "First, I gotta take care of some things."

Dana went back in the house with Endz in tow to find her phone and sent Neil a text.

Dana: *Endz wanted me to check out his new car. Will be back soon. The food is wrapped up in a plate in the refrigerator. Love you!*

After she sent the text, Dana fixed Neil's plate. Before wrapping up the rest of the lasagna in aluminum foil, she had an idea. "Are you hungry?" she asked Endz.

"As a motherfucker!" He rubbed his stomach.

"Well lucky for you, I just cooked." Dana grabbed some paper plates and the hot and cold bags. "We can eat some of this lasagna I cooked at our first stop; Turtle Park."

"Good looking out." Endz began to help Dana pack the food and drinks for their impromptu picnic in the park.

Chapter 35

"I'm home!" Neil announced as he waltzed through the door like everything was all good like he wasn't ignoring his pregnant fiancée's calls and texts because he was ball deep in Darnella's soaking wet pussy. "Dana baby! Where you at? I was held up at work." The lowdown nasty nigga already had his lie prepared and everything.

"Dana! Dana!" he continued to call out as he made his way up the stairs and into the master bedroom. Neil turned on the lights and expected to find Dana fast asleep in the bed, but instead, the bed was still made to perfection. Neil knew Dana wasn't in the bathroom because the door to the bathroom was wide opened and the lights inside were off.

While Neil was out doing him and expecting Dana to wait on him, the joke turned out to be on him. Dana wasn't even in the house.

What the fuck! "Where the fuck is that bitch!" Neil took his phone out of his pocket to see where the fuck Dana was. He then saw a text from her and read it out loud:

Dana: *Endz wanted me to check out his new car. Will be back soon. The food is wrapped up in a plate in the refrigerator. Love you!*

The thought of Dana with Endz was making Neil's blood boil. Dana was all his. He didn't give a fuck about Endz' boss status. Dana was his! Then something else donned on him. All that time they were separated, and Dana wouldn't tell him where she was staying. He finally figured out where she was hiding.

"That's where the fuck she was!" Neil paced back and forth seething with hot flaming fury. "She was with that motherfucking nigga this whole time! This whole motherfucking time!"

"See this is the shit her trifling ass be doing! Why the fuck can't that bitch act right?!" Neil stopped pacing back and forth like a psycho and he read the text message again. She also mentioned having a plate wrapped up for him. He figured no need to be pissed off on an empty stomach.

Neil calmed down enough to go back downstairs and into the kitchen. He took the plate out of the refrigerator and put it in the microwave. When the food was warm enough, he took the plate out of the microwave and grabbed a bottle of Pepsi from the refrigerator.

Neil took a seat with his plate at the dining room table and proceeded to eat his meal. "Mmmm! Delicious!" He continued to eat while trying to come up with an idea to fuck with Dana when she gets back.

*****

"I had a great time," Dana said while driving behind the wheel of Endz brand new car. She wanted to test drive the four-wheeled beauty on the way back home. "Thanks for taking me out and letting me drive your car."

"Anytime." Endz made himself comfortable in the passenger seat. "I had fun too and thanks for that meal. That lasagna was off the motherfucking chain!"

"Thank you and to be honest, I miss your cooking," Dana confessed.

Endz turned to Dana. "For real?"

"Yeah!" Dana smiled. "Don't tell me you don't know you be hooking it up in the kitchen."

Endz chucked and blushed. "That probably explains why every cook I've hired always quit within two weeks. That kind of thing happens when your grandmamma teaches you how to cook. You know my house is always open to you right." He reminded Dana.

"And that goes double for you." Endz rubbed Dana's pregnant belly. "Check this out." He pulled out his phone to show Dana a picture of a room in his house that was decorated into a pink princess nursery paradise.

"Endz!" Dana was blown away by the generous gesture.

194

"Yep." Endz put his phone back in his pocket. "Hooked it up so you and baby girl can always feel right at home."

"You didn't have to do this."

"I wanted to. You are my people and that means this baby is my people too," Endz insisted.

"Well, I..." Dana looked down at her belly ad giggled. "Correction, we appreciate you." They arrived at the house and Dana parked the car in the driveway.

Dana was about to open the car door, but Endz stopped her. "Allow me." He got out of the car. As he walked his sexy ass, smooth gentleman with solidified boss status to her car door, Dana thought to herself. *Such a gentleman! Why is this nigga single?*

Endz opened Dana's car door and helped her get out of the car. Normally, Dana was never the one to pry but she needed to know why this man does not have a woman. "I'm finally gonna ask. Why is your ass still single? Why hasn't any woman snatched your ass up yet?"

"Beats me?" He shrugged.

"I mean you are handsome, wealthy, have a great personality, loyal, a fine gentleman, and have a strong boss presence," Dana listed all of Endz attributes. "What the hell is the problem?"

"I don't know." Endz shrugged his shoulders and the two leaned on the side of his car. "My past relationships weren't meant to be. I just basically focused on work and taking care of my family."

"That's understandable." Dana nodded with understanding.

Endz stood in brief silence as something came over him. "Funny you should mention this because I have a question and maybe you can answer this from a woman's point of view."

"Sure. What's on your mind?" Endz smiled at Dana's eagerness to give him her undivided attention.

"Actually, I'm asking this for a friend."

"What's going on with your friend?" Dana asked with deep concern.

It was that sweet innocent nature that Endz always loved about Dana. He had to admit to himself that Miles was right. He was in love with Dana, but he couldn't tell her. So, he had to take the old tired ass 'asking for a friend' route.

"The thing is." Endz sighed. "My friend is single, and he's spent most of his life working and taking care of his family. He didn't give himself the opportunity to find love. He has this friend that he's very close to. She's a childhood friend. She's with another man."

"So, this friend of yours is starting to have strong feelings for this woman overtime during their adult years," Dana guessed.

"That's right," Endz confirmed. "He never crossed the line. That's not his style. He doesn't believe in going after another man's woman, so he suppresses his feelings out of respect for her relationship. What do you think?"

"This is some heavy shit!" Dana tried to answer Endz question the best way she could. "This friend of yours sounds like a loyal man. He doesn't want to do anything to alienate this woman. He might be the one for her because he's putting her feelings first. He cares about her feelings and her comfort. He doesn't want to do anything to jeopardize their friendship or her relationship with her man. Like they always say, anything can happen. Time will tell. If it's meant to be, it will happen naturally."

Endz took a moment to let Dana's words soak in before responding. "You make a lot of sense. I'll tell him to keep that in mind."

"You wanna come in for a minute?" Dana invited.

"Alright." Endz went on to follow Dana into the house.

Dana unlocked the door and she and Endz entered the house. She turned on the lights and was surprised to find Neil laying on the couch fast asleep. Endz closed the door behind him and that woke Neil up.

"Neil," Dana spoke. "I'm sorry, baby. I didn't know you were sleeping in here."

"It's okay, baby." Neil sat up and did a fake yawn. He was

never asleep. This was just another one of his manipulative acts. He couldn't risk beating the shit out of her like he wanted to right now, so he had to fuck with her in a much different approach.

"I was sitting here waiting for you. I must've lost track of the time and fell asleep." Neil wiped the fake sleep crust out of his eyes with the back of his hand. "Hey Endz. What's up?" He decided to drop the Mr. Washington formalities and switched to familiarity since the nigga is getting too close to his fiancée.

"What's up?" Endz gave a head nod.

"Where did y'all go?" Neil asked.

"Endz brought a new car and invited me to check it out and go for a ride," Dana answered.

"What kind go car did you get?" Neil already knew the answer to his own question because he took a peek out the window before executing his fake sleep trick.

"A midnight blue Rolls Royce."

Neil walked over to the window to take a look outside like he never saw the car before. "That car is sharp as fuck!" He was actually sincere. Neil really did think the car was off the chain.

"Isn't it?" Dana's expression of awe pissed Neil off a lot further, but he had to keep his cool and stick with his plan.

"I must've just missed your call when I came home. I got your message and I ate the food while I was sitting here waiting for you," Neil sounded all depressed trying to make Dana feel guilty about riding off with this boss nigga. "The food was delicious by the way."

"Yes, it was," Endz agreed with a smile.

"You ate some of it?" Neil asked with his eyes zeroed in at Endz.

"Yes, Dana did her thing. She packed some food for us before we left." Endz glanced at Dana. "We ate at Turtle Park and then went bowling."

"Really?" *She's giving this nigga my food?! These bitches ain't loyal!* Neil seethed on the inside.

Endz phone started to ring and he pulled it out of his pocket.

"Excuse me." He stepped into the dining room for some privacy to answer the call.

"I'm sorry I missed your call." Dana walked over to Neil to hug him.

"It's okay baby," Neil said with warmth and understanding.

"I wanna make it up to you."

Gotcha bitch! "Okay baby."

The two shared a deep passionate kiss. They were lost in their loving passion until they heard Endz's footsteps along with his serious voice. "Sorry to interrupt, but Dana I think you better come with me."

"What's wrong, Endz?" His serious facial expression got Dana's attention.

"That was Miles, I was talking to. Dominique is a mess and she's gonna need you right now," Endz said.

"What's wrong with her?" Dana asked.

Endz didn't know how he was gonna say what he needed to say. All he could do was just be a man and deliver the news straight. "Patresha is dead."

"What?!" Dana and Neil both exclaimed with shock.

"Yes, apparently she committed suicide," Endz reported.

"Oh my God!" Dana knew Dominique must be in shambles at this very moment. Losing a close sibling unexpectedly is tragic. Dana remembered how she felt when got the news that Eli was murdered. Dominique was there for her during that difficult time. Now it's time for Dana to do the same for Dominique. "Dominique must be devastated. I gotta go over there."

"I'll drive you over there," Neil offered his support.

"Thanks, Neil," Dana said with appreciation. The three left the house and jumped into their vehicles. Neil and Dana followed Endz to Miles and Dominique's house to comfort them in their time of need. Unaware that they are being accompanied by the reason behind Patresha's suicide and the fucked-up part is that he is fully aware that he is the cause of her demise.

Chapter 36

"Why would she do this? Why the fuck would she do this!?" Dominique's face was covered with tears with her body all balled up on the couch in the living room.

"I'm so sorry, baby." Miles had his arms wrapped around Dominique trying to comfort her. It was futile, but he wanted to show his wife that she didn't have to go through this unbearable pain alone.

Ring! Ring!

Miles got off the couch to answer the door. "Hey what's up y'all. Thanks for coming," he greeted Endz, Dana, and Neil and let them inside the house.

"Of course!" Endz gave his baby cousin a manly hug.

Dana saw her best friend on the couch in a million pieces. "Dominique."

Dominique looked up with her blood-shot red swollen eyes. "Oh, Dana!"

Dana slowly walked over to Dominique to hold her in her arms tightly. "I'm so sorry. I came the second Endz told me."

"Thanks, Dana," Dominique said between sobs. "I can't believe she would do this. I thought she was happy. How in the fuck could I have been so motherfucking blind? I should've..."

"Don't do that to yourself." Dana didn't want Dominique blaming herself for this tragedy. "There was nothing anybody could've done."

"How did this happen?" Endz asked.

Dominique was about to answer Endz's question, but she couldn't even say the words. She was too grief-stricken, so Miles went ahead to answer on her behalf. "Lexus and Wyatt found Patresha's body on the bathroom floor. She overdosed on some pills and every medication she had within reach."

"Shit!" Dana shook her head with pity.

"Lexus is really torn up about this," Miles said. "I called her father. He's coming first thing tomorrow morning. Lexus' brother, sister-in-law, and cousin are on the next plane here.

We're gonna set up the guesthouse for them."

"How is Chase dealing with this?" Dana asked because she remembered Chase was a respectable young man who put Patresha on a very high pedestal.

"Lexus's father, August, said he's extremely devastated. Chase doesn't understand how this could've happened. He was really looking forward to him and Patresha building their lives together." Miles felt sorry for the young man. Losing the woman that he loved just when their relationship was starting to blossom.

"Poor kid." Endz shook his head.

Little pussy ass nigga! Neil chuckled at Chase's expense on the inside. "It's very terrible. I can't imagine what he's going through." He walked over to Dominique to hug her. "I'm sorry for your loss, Dominique." He kissed her cheek.

"Thanks, Neil," Dominique said with appreciation and returned Neil's hug.

"I know it hurts." Neil rubbed Dominique's back as he held her in his arms. "It's gonna be okay."

"What the fuck am I gonna do?!" Dominique cried out as she gently released herself from Neil's embrace and fell back into Dana's arms. "That's my motherfucking baby sister! That's my motherfucking heart! Dana, will you please stay with me?" she pleaded with her swollen tear-filled eyes.

"Of course!" Dana turned to Neil and asked. "You don't mind, do you? I can't leave her like this."

"Baby, I understand." Neil rubbed Dana's back and kissed her lips. "Dominique needs you right now. I just can't understand what would drive a nice, sweet, young girl to this point."

"It's a mystery." Dana sighed. "Thanks for being under-standing and caring. You're so sweet." She hugged and kissed Neil.

"Anything for you, baby." Neil did a great job keeping up the supportive sympathetic man charade. "I'm gonna head out and you call me if you need anything. Okay, baby."

"Alright baby. I love you." Dana kissed Neil.
"I love you too." Neil turned to everyone and said, "Good-night everyone and, again, my condolences."
Ding-dong, the nasty, fat, sloppy bitch is dead!

Jamila

Chapter 37

Everyone gathered at Union Baptist Church for Patresha's homegoing services. This has been a difficult week filled with grief and questions. Miles and Dominique welcomed Lexus's family into their home with opened arms and setup the guesthouse for them. Lexus suggested Aiesha sing *Dreaming of You* by Selena.

The church was packed with Albany State University students, faculty, family, and friends paying their respects. Patresha was lying in a lavender casket dressed in an elegant purple dress. Everyone was taking their seats waiting for the funeral to start. Lexus, Wyatt, Chase, and Be-vo were all sitting together. Be-vo with his cornrows freshly done and letting his beard grow out made him almost pass for Nipsey Hussle. Lexus and Chase have been crying nonstop all week. Wyatt held Lexus close to him.

"Thank you so much for coming," Miles said to the young people with Dominique standing next to him obviously still torn up.

"We appreciate it," Dominique said trying to keep her composure. "I know y'all loved her."

"Yes, we did," Be-vo said. "I'm sorry for your loss."

"Thanks, Bellamy," Dominique hugged Be-vo. The grief was so thick Be-vo didn't even bother correcting Dominique about his name.

Dominique glanced at Lexus and pulled her into her arms. "It's gonna be okay, sweetheart. Thanks for being a good friend to my baby sister."

"Of course, Dominique," Lexus said. "She was my sister too."

Dominique hugged Wyatt and said. "Thank you and you take care of Lexus here, okay?"

"Of course," Wyatt said. "And I'm sorry for your loss."

Dominique looked over at Chase who looked like his whole world was taken from him. "Chase."

Chase looked up at Dominique. "Yes."

"You really loved her, didn't you?"

"Yes, I did. I can't believe she's gone."

"Chase look at me." Chase looked into Dominique's eyes. "I know Patresha meant the world to you. Thank you for showing her how a real man loves a woman." She hugged him and went on to say, "At least I can take comfort in that. Thank you."

Miles and Dominique went to the front to take their seats. "How could it get any worse than this?" Be-vo sighed.

Wyatt looked back at the church entrance and his eyes stretched with disbelief. "I think it just did."

"What are you talking about?" Chase asked.

"That motherfucker!" Be-vo hissed through his teeth.

Lexus didn't even have to turn around to see what Wyatt and Be-vo were talking about, but she turned around anyway. She couldn't believe who just walked through the door. It was Neil holding Dana's hand. *This motherfucker had the audacity to show his sorry ass face here! Talk about a lack of respect and immorality!*

"This nigga has to be either stupid, crazy, the devil, or all of the above!" Lexus hated Neil with a passion after what he put Patresha through.

"I can't believe Neil is here," Wyatt said.

Hearing Neil's name being mentioned caused a reaction in Chase. "That's Neil?"

"Yes," Be-vo confirmed.

"I'm gonna fuck this nigga up!" Chase jumped out of his seat. Be-vo had to literally pull Chase back in his seat.

"Chase, I know you wanna kick his ass right now and trust and believe we all wanna join you, but now is not the time." Be-vo tried to calm him down. "This is Patresha's day. Don't let Neil fuck it up, okay?"

"Okay." Chase didn't calm down completely. Just enough to not cause a scene.

Lexus's blood began to boil as she was having flashbacks of how many times that she'd witnessed Neil dogging Patresha out.

Her heart began to beat rapidly as she clenched her fists. Wyatt had to hold Lexus with his arms tightly to keep her from shaking and prevent her from emotionally exploding. Meanwhile, Be-vo kept a close eye on an anger-filled Chase. Wyatt and Be-vo had an important job to do. The job was to keep the two cousins' emotions in check during the ceremony which was about to start.

*****

After the ceremony was over, everybody began to walk out of the church to give the family and close friends their support before departing. Neil and Dana approached Dominique and Miles. Dana hugged Dominique consoling her. Lexus was nearby with her family and was staring Neil down with murder in her eyes. She was seconds away from catching a case.

"I'm so sorry, Dominique," Dana said.

"Thanks for being here for me, girl," Dominique said.

"It's gonna be okay, Dominique," Neil said, trying to sound supportive. "She's in a better place now. We'll get through this difficult time together as a family."

Hearing Neil say that bullshit, did it for Lexus. She spun around and charged towards Neil and got in his face. "She's in a better place? Motherfucker, you're the reason she's gone! You beat her like a punching bag! You scarred her mentally, physically, and emotionally. Now you talking all this bullshit about she's in a better place. Nigga, fuck you!" Lexus yelled before spitting in his face.

"Excuse me?" Dominique wanted to know what the fuck was going on and she wanted to know right motherfucking now. "Lexus, what are you talking about?"

"Neil seduced Patresha and used and abused her!" Lexus blurted out. "He called her fat and all kinds of bitches and hoes and shit! He stood her up and let his side hoes embarrass her like at the club and I had to stomp that hoe's ass! I had to pick her up after he left her stranded and made her walk in the rain because she found out he made that hoe Sarina crash into her car and beat her up and took her out to eat instead!"

It all started to come back to Dana. The exact same flowers Patresha's secret admirer gave her. Her confrontation with Darnella when she mentioned a fat girl that Neil dogged out at the club. The only Sarina she knew was Neil's therapist.

"I knew it!" Domonique yelled. "I knew you wasn't shit!" She lunged for Neil, but Miles held her back. "You killed my sister!"

"I don't know what the fuck you talking about," Neil defended. "You're gonna really believe an obvious crazy little girl rambling about nothing." He pointed at Lexus.

Chase rolled up on Neil and got in his face. "Don't you ever talk about my cousin like that you fuck nigga!"

Neil laughed at Chase like he was a joke. "Oh, take your little virgin ass on somewhere."

Chase was about to lunge for Neil, but Wyatt and Be-vo pulled him away. "Come on! He's not worth it!"

Neil tried to play it off like he didn't just get exposed. "Come on Dana. Let's go."

Dana didn't budge. She just asked one question. "Neil, how did you know that Chase was a virgin?" She didn't need an answer. She already figured it out. She mentioned the Miami trip to Neil. This nigga hasn't changed at all. He was still the lying, abusive, dirty bastard he always been. "I can't do this anymore," was all Dana could say and left Neil looking stupid all by himself.

As Dana walked away, she took off her engagement ring. She stopped by a large gathering of Patresha's classmates and yelled at them. "Hey catch!" And threw her engagement ring into the crowd. She giggled to herself at the liberating spectacle she just created of broke college students fighting over an engagement ring that costs about five times their whole tuition.

206

Chapter 38

I'm so fucking stupid! Dana thought during her Uber ride back to the house. She felt like a complete fool thinking Neil could change. Not only was he not a changed man, but he took complete advantage of an innocent and vulnerable young girl, tearing her to shreds. Dana was officially done with Neil. She was gonna pack her shit and start a new life with her baby. She never pictured herself as a single mother, but it is what it is. Besides the only good thing that Neil brought into her life was this sweet little bundle of joy growing inside her.

Dana pulled out her phone and called Endz. "Hey, baby girl! Are you okay? I saw what went down at the funeral."

"I'd be lying if I said I was okay, but I'm not. Listen, I need to move back in with you until I get on my feet," Dana said.

"Girl, you know you can stay with me forever." Dana chuckled at Endz's comment. "I already got the moving trucks waiting for you." He knew after what went down with Neil at the funeral Dana would need help moving out as soon as possible.

"Thanks, Endz. I knew I could count on you." Dana cracked a smile sounding hopeful. "You know I got you, baby girl," Endz said. "I'll be waiting for you at home."

"Alright, I'll see you later. Bye-bye!"

"Bye-bye, baby girl!" Endz said before ending the call.

When Dana arrived at the house, she saw the moving trucks parked in the driveway. She thanked the Uber driver before getting out of the car. She greeted the moving men and let them inside the house. She gave them instructions on what to pack and take to Endz's house.

As the moving men were working Dana went on to pack her suitcases. As the moving men were loading up the trucks, Dana loaded up her car until she couldn't anymore. When the moving men were finished, Dana thanked them for their services, and they went on their way. Dana went back into the house to pack her last bag in the bedroom. She grabbed her stuffed pink dinosaur, her most treasured possession, and put it in the bag.

All of the sudden, Neil appeared out of nowhere obviously flabbergasted at the sight of Dana packing her things.

"Dana! What the fuck do you think you are doing?" Neil asked with anger in his voice while witnessing his fiancée and the mother of his unborn child zipping up her last bag in the master bedroom they no longer share together.

"What the fuck does it look like I'm doing?" Dana barked out her answer and grabbed her bag. "I'm packing my shit and leaving your ass! Something I should've done a long time ago!" She brushed past Neil and walked out the door and down the stairs.

"Stop being so fucking overly dramatic so we can talk about this!" Neil ordered as he followed Dana down the stairs.

"We ain't got shit to talk about!" Dana's mind was completely made up. She was officially done with this nigga's abuse, lies, deceits, deceptions, disrespect, and community dick. There was no changing her mind. She had reached her breaking point with this abusive fuck boy that she had no business giving a second of her time to. "That shit you pulled was unforgivable!"

Neil grabbed Dana's arm firmly. "And I told your ass I was sorry!"

Dana snatched her arm away from Neil's tight grip. "You only sorry that your no-good ass got caught! This is it! I'm done! It's over! I'm leaving your motherfucking ass and I'm taking my baby with me!" She referred to the seven-month-old fetus growing inside of her.

Whap!

Neil gave Dana a hard back-handed slap making her fall on the floor and drop her bag. "You ain't going nowhere! You understand that shit, bitch!"

Neil pounced on top of Dana and started beating her like she was a man. He punched her repeatedly in the face and all over her body.

"Stop! Please stop!" Dana tried to block the blows with her arms but to no avail. Neil's rage was in autopilot.

Neil grabbed Dana by her hair and screamed in her face. "Shut the fuck up! You ungrateful bitch!" And delivered another punch to her right eye.

"Stop! I'm carrying our baby!" Neil ignored Dana's desperate pleas for her and her unborn baby's life by continuing to beat her like she was less than nothing.

Dana leaned over on her left side in pain and Neil began to kick her in the chest and back. "You wanna leave me!"

Kick!

"Huh!" After a few more kicks Neil stopped kicking Dana. He caught his breath and came up with a devilish idea. "If you wanna leave that motherfucking bad go ahead and leave then bitch! I'll even drop your worthless hoe ass off!" He yanked Dana off the floor. "Now take off your clothes!"

What the fuck? Dana had no idea Neil was this crazy, but then again maybe she should've known by the obvious red flags throughout their entire relationship. "Neil please don't..."

Neil cut her off with another pimp slap to the face. "Bitch take off your motherfucking clothes now!" Neil let Dana go and she managed to maintain her balance. She was quivering with fear as she began to undress. "Hurry your dumb ass up!" Dana picked up the pace until her naked and bruised body was completely exposed.

"Let's go!" Neil yanked Dana's arm and dragged her towards the front door.

"Where are we going?" Dana stuttered with fright.

Neil answered Dana's question by slamming her head on the coffee table knocking her out. He dragged Dana outside and threw her body in the trunk of his car. He got in his driver's seat and went on to his destination. It took about thirty minutes for Neil to find the perfect spot. He found a path that led to the woods and followed it. When he felt like he was deep enough in the forest Neil stopped the car.

Neil got out and popped the trunk. Dana was still unconscious. He picked up Dana's body and threw her towards the trees like he was disposing of some trash.

Jamila

"Good riddance bitch!" Neil chuckled and got back in his car and drove off like nothing happened as the rain started to pour down.

Chapter 39

"How is she, Kiriakis?" Miles' mother Ruby asked him. She is the only person he can't object to calling him by his government. They were gathered at Miles and Dominique's house. Dominique was in the master bedroom being comforted by Momma Flo.

"She's still trying to process all of this." Miles sighed. "I don't know how I'm gonna help her through this."

"All you can do is be there for her." Miles's stepfather Oliver said.

Miles really treasured the relationship he had with Oliver. He's been more of a father to him than his sperm donor. Miles's biological father was the type of man who couldn't keep his dick in his pants if his life depended on it. The last straw was when Ruby was pregnant with their second child. They were expecting a girl. She ended up having a miscarriage because she contracted chlamydia. It was so bad it messed up her reproductive system and she couldn't have any more children.

That was the end of their marriage. Miles was eight years old. Two years later, Ruby met Oliver. Oliver made Ruby happy and showed her that she was the only woman he needed, wanted, and desired. Of course, when Miles's biological father found out Ruby was with another man, he got in his feelings and distanced himself from Miles. It didn't matter with Miles anyway. It wasn't like he was much use when he was around anyway.

"I gotta go get the house ready for Dana," Endz said. "I'll be back." Endz gave Miles dap. "See you, Unc." He gave Oliver a manly hug. "Bye Aunt Ruby." He hugged and kissed Ruby on the cheek.

"Take care of yourself, Nicky," Ruby said. "I'm gonna check on Dominique and take momma back to the home."

After Miles saw everybody out of the house and checked on Lexus and her people at the guest house, he went upstairs to check on Dominique. He found her in their bed holding a picture of her and Patresha when they were little girls in her arms like it was a teddy bear. Miles didn't know what to say or do except join her in bed and wrap his muscular protective arms around her.

"I knew it!" Dominique said. "I knew that fucking bastard wasn't shit!"

"Don't you worry, baby. He won't get away with this. Dana is done with him," Miles assured his grieving wife. "She's gonna move in with Endz."

"Good." Domonique nodded her head. "Now she'll be with a real man."

"I don't think she's ready for that yet," Miles said. "But I know deep down Endz wants her."

Dominique sat up and wiped her tears with the back of her hand. "Right! Right! It'll happen naturally. It's their destiny." The two laid in bed with their arms around each other in silence thinking about the events that occurred at Patresha's funeral.

Ring! Ring!

"I'll get it." Miles got out of bed. "It's probably Endz." He assumed and exited the bedroom to answer the front door.

Dominique still laid in bed in silence with a blank look on her face. All of a sudden Miles came back into the bedroom with a look on his face that read 'I can't believe this shit!' The look on Miles' face made Dominique ask. "Baby, what's the matter?"

Miles put his hands up preparing for the unexpected. "Baby, I know you're very emotional right now, but don't get mad."

Dominique leaped like a frog out of bed on her feet the second Miles said that. Knowing damn well anytime somebody says 'don't get mad' that's exactly what the fuck they gonna do. "What the hell?!"

"Dominique!" a woman's voice was heard calling from downstairs.

"Oh, fuck no!" Dominique knew exactly who that voice belonged to. She Sonic-dashed downstairs and into the living room. She found the woman that she heard call her name and she was right about whose voice it was. "What the fuck do you want Kate?!" She gave a hate-filled bitter greeting to the woman who gave birth to her.

"I was at Patresha's funeral," Kate said. "I wanted to be here for you."

"Bitch fuck you!" Dominique yelled with scorn with Miles holding her back. "Your ass didn't give a fuck when she was alive, so why give a fuck now!"

"I'm sorry, baby. I wanna make it right!" Katie pleaded with regret.

"Too late and too bad! Get the fuck out my face, bitch!"

"Kate, I think you better leave." Miles tried to be polite. Kate couldn't do anything but turn around and walk out the door.

"The nerve of that motherfucking bitch!" Dominique said. "Coming up in here like she's Mother of the Year after all these years and everything she's put us through. Fuck that bitch!"

*****

Eight Years Earlier

"Dominique! I'm finished with my homework." Ten-year-old. Patresha handed seventeen-year-old Dominique her math homework.

"Okay, sweetie! Let's see how we did," Dominique grabbed Patresha's math homework and started to look over it. Since their egg donor, Kate was too bitter to perform her motherly responsibilities Dominique had to take on the role of Patresha's mother with their grandmother's guidance.

"Good job girl!" Dominique gave Patresha a big hug.

The door opened and Kate's live-in boyfriend Dario entered the house. Dominique and Patresha tried to stay out of his way. Dominique couldn't stand his ass. He wasn't about shit. One day, she saw Dario kissing another woman on her way home from her part-time job at a used car lot. She told Kate, but all she did was accuse Dominique of lying and not wanting her to be happy and all that other dumb ass bullshit.

Actually, Dominique didn't give two fucks. Kate stopped

213

being viewed as a mom to her eyes since she was ten years old. But Kate did give her this gift called life, so Dominique did feel obligated to tell her about her nasty ass cheating boyfriend. Dominique told her grandmother about it and she followed her advice. Tell her one time and whatever she does with the information is up to her.

"Hey girls!" Dario greeted.

"Hello!" Dominique and Patresha greeted him to be polite.

Dominique turned her focus back to Patresha. "What's next?"

"I have a spelling test to study for." Patresha handed Dominique a piece of paper. "Here are the words and definitions."

"Dominique, I need to talk to you," Dario said.

Dominique sighed with annoyance. "Patresha go ahead and get started studying for the test. I'll be right back to check on you."

"Okay Dominique," Patresha said and went to her studies as Dario followed Dominique into her bedroom.

"Alright what is..." Dominique was cut off by Dario's tongue in her mouth. "Nigga, what the fuck are you doing!" she screamed and struggled to get out of his arms.

"Girl, you know you want it!" Dario threw Dominique on the bed and pounced on top of her.

"Help! Somebody help me!" Dominique screamed and tried to get away.

"Shut the fuck up and take this dick!" Dario growled and backhanded her. He yanked his dick out of his sweatpants and reached under her dress to tear off her panties.

"No! Stop! Please!" Dominique screamed.

Dario was about to slap her again, but Patresha ran into the room and kicked the side of his leg as hard as she could. Dario rolled over in pain giving Dominique and Patresha the chance to escape into the living room where they bumped into Kate. "What the fuck is going on?" she yelled.

"Dario tried to rape me!" Dominique was shaken.

214

"That's not true!" Dario appeared while fixing his sweat-pants obviously trying to put his dick back up. "She came on to me and it was a moment of weakness. Baby please forgive me, baby!" he pleaded to Kate.

"You lying, nasty, hoe!" Kate snapped at Dominique.

"Why the fuck am I not surprised?" Dominique rolled her eyes and scoffed at Kate. She was disappointed but not surprised.

"It's true, momma." Patresha tried to stand up for Dominique by telling the truth about what really happened. "Dario tried to hurt her."

"Shut your little fat ass up!" Dario yelled at Patresha.

"He's right! Stay out of it Letresha!" Kate foolishly agreed with Dario.

"Patresha!" she corrected.

"You don't even know your own child's name." Dominique hated Kate by the minute.

"I need to go!" Dario kissed Kate before he walked out the door. "I'll be back." He slammed the door behind him.

"Nasty perverted ass nigga!" Dominique yelled out as the door slammed.

"Don't you ever talk about my man like that!" Kate screamed in Dominique's face. "I knew your hoe ass would pull this shit someday. You've done nothing but ruin my motherfucking life!"

"I've been hearing this bullshit for seventeen motherfucking years!" Dominique was fed up. "I am sick of you blaming me and Patresha for the reason you're so miserable! It ain't our fault. Whatever the fuck your problem is, suck it up and get the fuck over it! You're such a miserable dumb ass bitch no wonder daddy and Carl left your ass!"

Having Dominique and Patresha's biological fathers leaving being thrown in Kate's face made her snap and she slapped Dominique hard across the face.

Dominique took a brief moment to rub her right cheek where she got slapped at. She then returned the slap, but twice as hard.

Jamila

Soon the already strained mother and daughter relationship turned into a brutal melee. Punches were thrown. Hair pulling. Kicking, screaming, and scratching each other's eyes out.

"Nasty ass little hoe!" Kate punched Dominique in the eye and wrapped her hands around her throat.

"Dumb ass bitch!" Dominique kneed Kate in the stomach.

"Y'all break it up." Dominique and Patresha's grandmother pulled the ladies apart. Patresha called her, told her what was going on, and let her in the house.

"Get out!" Kate started daggers at Dominique. "Pack your shit and get your trifling, worthless, slut ass the fuck out of my house!"

Dominique and Patresha went to pack their things. Their grandmother didn't want either of her precious granddaughters living under that roof with that sick fuck and decided to take them in. She looked down at her sad and pitiful daughter, telling her, "One day you're gonna regret this." And eight years later that day came.

Chapter 40
1998

"Here you go, mommy!" A cute little five-year-old boy handed his beautiful dark-skinned mother a tissue to wipe away her tears.

"Thanks, Neil." The beautiful woman hugged her son and wiped her tears with the tissue.

Neil looked at his mother's busted lip. "I don't like it when he hurts you."

The beautiful woman sighed. "I don't like it either baby, but I love him. I wish he would change." Neil's father was a very abusive man. He was like Dr. Jekyll and Mr. Hyde. Some days, he was the perfect husband and father, and other days, he was worse than Satan.

He wasn't home now. He took off after he beat his wife just because another man complimented her appearance and she smiled. This was odd because less than twenty-four hours before the beating she caught him kissing another woman in the car.

The battered woman held Neil tight. "Neil, can you promise me something, baby?"

"Yes, momma?"

"Promise me that you'll be a good boy and grow up to be a good man. I want you to never do anything to hurt girls, okay?" The woman wanted to make sure that Neil didn't turn out anything like his father.

"Yes, momma."

She gave Neil a big hug and kiss on the cheek. "That's my sweet little boy."

"Abby!"

Abby and Neil jumped at the sound of her husband's voice. He had a bouquet of red roses and a wrapped-up present in his hand. Abby was petrified with fear.

"Neil go to your room. I need to talk to your mother alone," he said to his son like he was the perfect father.

"Okay," Neil said. He carefully walked past his father and

left his parents' bedroom.

When Neil was out of sight, his father flashed a charming smile and handed his guilt gifts to Abby. "Baby, I'm so sorry."

"Why do you keep doing this to me?" Abby cried. "What is it about me that gets you so angry? Am I enough for you?"

"Baby, it's not you," he pleaded. "I don't know what came over me. You know I love you?"

"I don't know how much of this I can take." Abby shook her head. "The beating and the cheating..."

"She meant nothing to me." He cut her off with the classic excuse for cheating line. "I only want you. I'm a changed man. You believe me, don't you?"

Abby sighed. "I want to believe you."

"Then believe me."

Abby didn't know what to do or say. She desperately wanted to believe in her husband. "Will you promise me that you will never hit me and cheat on me again?"

"Baby, I promise," he said sincerely before pulling Abby into a kiss. "I love you."

"I love you too."

*****

Neil stood over his mother's grave. The tombstone read 'Here Lies Abigail 'Abby' Reese Malone-Henderson.' He took a brief moment of silence and stared at the tombstone. "Fuck you, bitch!" And fired a huge loogie straight at her tombstone and stomped to his car and drove off.

The moment Neil was out of sight, a man who looked like an older version of Matt Barnes walked towards the grave. He took a disinfectant wipe out of his pocket and wiped away the spit Neil left behind on the tombstone. He looked back at the direction that Neil drove off. He looked at the tombstone and busted out crying. "What did I do? What the fuck did I do!"

Chapter 41

On the way home, Neil felt like he was the shit! Patresha was six feet deep and Dana's ungrateful ass was rotting in the woods somewhere butt naked with rain falling down on her nude body. That'll teach her not to leave him just like his mother did.

Neil arrived at his house and was met with an unexpected surprise. He found Endz parked in his driveway sitting on the hood of his brand-new Rolls Royce waiting patiently for something like he had all the time in the world.

"What the fuck does this nigga want?" Neil rolled his eyes before parking the car. He got out and walked towards Endz. "What's up, Endz?"

"Hey, Neil. How you doing?" Endz greeted back. "May I come in?"

"Sure." Neil opened the door and the two men went inside. "What can I do for you?"

"Have you seen Dana? We were supposed to have a meeting this morning and she never showed up." End wondered with concern.

"Oh, she went shopping. We're going on vacation," Neil lied through his motherfucking teeth.

"Without her car?" Endz raised his eyebrow as he took note of Dana's fully loaded car still parked outside.

"She decided to take one of my cars." Neil thought on his feet.

"I see." Endz nodded. "Where are y'all going for y'all vacation?"

"We're going to the Grand Canyon. We need to get away from it all and clear our minds. We need to get away from all these false allegations," Neil explained.

"Yeah, I hope it all works out for y'all." Endz shared Neil's hopes. "Don't worry, all of this will clear up and the truth will come out."

"Thanks, man." Neil sighed with relief.

"Anytime," Endz said as he headed for the door. "You keep

your head up and when you see Dana, tell her to give me a call."

"I will," Neil said.

"I'll let myself out," Endz said as he walked out of the house.

Neil closed the door behind Endz and felt like he dodged a huge bullet. Completely oblivious to the fact that Endz walked out of the house with Dana's purse and bag with the head of her stuffed pink dinosaur sticking out.

*****

"That arrogant motherfucker!" Endz busted in Dana's hospital room at Phoebe Putney Memorial Hospital looking like he was ready to go to war. Dominique and Miles were sitting by Dana's bedside.

Endz dropped Dana's purse and bag in an empty chair. He knew Dana would never leave her stuffed pink dinosaur behind. Finding that and listening to Neil's bullshit story told him everything he needed to know. Actually, he already knew everything. He was just playing dumb because he wanted to see how far Neil was gonna take this lie.

"Why didn't you tell us?" Dominique's watery eyes looked at Dana. "We would've helped you! We would've taken you away from that nigga!"

Endz walked over to Dana's bedside. He grabbed her hand and kissed it. "I need you to come back to us, baby girl."

"Dana please wake up!" Dominique pleaded with Miles cradling her. "That nigga already took Patresha away from me. He can't take you away from me too!"

Beep! Beep!

"Oh shit!" Miles shrieked as the machines connected to Dana's body started to go off.

The doctors and nurses busted into the room. "Everybody out! We need everyone out stat!"

They didn't have to tell them twice. Endz, Miles, and Dominique hurried out of the room. While they were in the

220

hallway, one of the doctors was heard yelling, "We're losing her!"

"What the fuck!" Endz shouted. "Dana! Dana!" he cried out loud and Miles and Dominique tried to console him. "I can't lose her! I love her! That motherfucker is gonna pay for this shit!" Endz officially declared war on Neil.

One of the doctors walked out of the room and walked up to Endz, Dominique, and Miles. "What's going on, Doctor?" Miles asked.

The doctor sighed before giving his answer. "Well..."

TO BE CONTINUED...
Into the Arms of His Boss 2
Coming Soon

Submission Guideline

Submit the first three chapters of your completed manu-script to ldpsubmissions@gmail.com, subject line: Your book's title. The manuscript must be in a .doc file and sent as an attachment. Document should be in Times New Roman, double spaced and in size 12 font. Also, provide your synopsis and full contact information. If sending multiple submissions, they must each be in a separate email.

Have a story but no way to send it electronically? You can still submit to LDP/Ca$h Presents. Send in the first three chapters, written or typed, of your completed manuscript to:

LDP: Submissions Dept
Po Box 944
Stockbridge, Ga 30281

DO NOT send original manuscript. Must be a duplicate.

Provide your synopsis and a cover letter containing your full contact information.

Thanks for considering LDP and Ca$h Presents.

Into the Arms of His Boss

Coming Soon from Lock Down Publications/Ca$h Presents

BOW DOWN TO MY GANGSTA

By **Ca$h**

TORN BETWEEN TWO

By **Coffee**

THE STREETS STAINED MY SOUL **II**

By **Marcellus Allen**

BLOOD OF A BOSS **VI**

SHADOWS OF THE GAME II

By **Askari**

LOYAL TO THE GAME **IV**

By **T.J. & Jelissa**

IF LOVING YOU IS WRONG... **III**

By **Jelissa**

TRUE SAVAGE **VII**

MIDNIGHT CARTEL III

DOPE BOY MAGIC IV

CITY OF KINGZ II

By **Chris Green**

BLAST FOR ME **III**

A SAVAGE DOPEBOY III

CUTTHROAT MAFIA III

By **Ghost**

A HUSTLER'S DECEIT III

KILL ZONE **II**

BAE BELONGS TO ME III

A DOPE BOY'S QUEEN III

By **Aryanna**

COKE KINGS V

223

Jamila

KING OF THE TRAP II

By **T.J. Edwards**

GORILLAZ IN THE BAY V

3X KRAZY II

De'Kari

THE STREETS ARE CALLING II

Duquie Wilson

KINGPIN KILLAZ IV

STREET KINGS III

PAID IN BLOOD III

CARTEL KILLAZ IV

DOPE GODS III

Hood Rich

SINS OF A HUSTLA II

ASAD

KINGZ OF THE GAME VI

Playa Ray

SLAUGHTER GANG IV

RUTHLESS HEART IV

By Willie Slaughter

THE HEART OF A SAVAGE III

By Jibril Williams

FUK SHYT II

By Blakk Diamond

THE REALEST KILLAZ III

By Tranay Adams

TRAP GOD III

By Troublesome

YAYO IV

GHOST MOB

Into the Arms of His Boss

Stilloan Robinson
KINGPIN DREAMS III
By Paper Boi Rari
CREAM II
By Yolanda Moore
SON OF A DOPE FIEND III
By Renta
FOREVER GANGSTA II
GLOCKS ON SATIN SHEETS III
By Adrian Dulan
LOYALTY AIN'T PROMISED III
By Keith Williams
THE PRICE YOU PAY FOR LOVE II
By Destiny Skai
CONFESSIONS OF A GANGSTA II
By Nicholas Lock
I'M NOTHING WITHOUT HIS LOVE II
SINS OF A THUG II
By Monet Dragun
LIFE OF A SAVAGE IV
A GANGSTA'S QUR'AN III
MURDA SEASON III
GANGLAND CARTEL II
By **Romell Tukes**
QUIET MONEY III
THUG LIFE II
By **Trai'Quan**
THE STREETS MADE ME III
By **Larry D. Wright**
THE ULTIMATE SACRIFICE VI

Jamila

IF YOU CROSS ME ONCE II

ANGEL III

By **Anthony Fields**

FRIEND OR FOE III

By **Mimi**

SAVAGE STORMS II

By **Meesha**

BLOOD ON THE MONEY II

By J-Blunt

THE STREETS WILL NEVER CLOSE II

By K'ajji

NIGHTMARES OF A HUSTLA II

By King Dream

THE WIFEY I USED TO BE II

By Nicole Goosby

INTO THE ARM OF HIS BOSS

By Jamila

<u>Available Now</u>

RESTRAINING ORDER **I & II**

By **CA$H & Coffee**

LOVE KNOWS NO BOUNDARIES **I II & III**

By **Coffee**

RAISED AS A GOON I, II, III & IV

BRED BY THE SLUMS I, II, III

BLAST FOR ME I & II

ROTTEN TO THE CORE I II III

A BRONX TALE I, II, III

DUFFEL BAG CARTEL I II III IV

HEARTLESS GOON I II III IV

Into the Arms of His Boss

A SAVAGE DOPEBOY I II

HEARTLESS GOON I II III

DRUG LORDS I II III

CUTTHROAT MAFIA I II

By **Ghost**

LAY IT DOWN **I & II**

LAST OF A DYING BREED

BLOOD STAINS OF A SHOTTA I & II III

By **Jamaica**

LOYAL TO THE GAME I II III

LIFE OF SIN I, II III

By **TJ & Jelissa**

BLOODY COMMAS I & II

SKI MASK CARTEL I II & III

KING OF NEW YORK I II,III IV V

RISE TO POWER I II III

COKE KINGS I II III IV

BORN HEARTLESS I II III IV

KING OF THE TRAP

By **T.J. Edwards**

IF LOVING HIM IS WRONG…I & II

LOVE ME EVEN WHEN IT HURTS I II III

By **Jelissa**

WHEN THE STREETS CLAP BACK I & II III

THE HEART OF A SAVAGE I II

By **Jibril Williams**

A DISTINGUISHED THUG STOLE MY HEART I II & III

LOVE SHOULDN'T HURT I II III IV

RENEGADE BOYS I II III IV

PAID IN KARMA I II III

Jamila

SAVAGE STORMS

By **Meesha**

A GANGSTER'S CODE I &, II III

A GANGSTER'S SYN I II III

THE SAVAGE LIFE I II III

CHAINED TO THE STREETS I II III

BLOOD ON THE MONEY

By J-Blunt

PUSH IT TO THE LIMIT

By **Bre' Hayes**

BLOOD OF A BOSS **I, II, III, IV, V**

SHADOWS OF THE GAME

By **Askari**

THE STREETS BLEED MURDER **I, II & III**

THE HEART OF A GANGSTA I II& III

By **Jerry Jackson**

CUM FOR ME I II III IV V VI

An **LDP Erotica Collaboration**

BRIDE OF A HUSTLA **I II & II**

THE FETTI GIRLS **I, II& III**

CORRUPTED BY A GANGSTA I, II III, IV

BLINDED BY HIS LOVE

THE PRICE YOU PAY FOR LOVE

DOPE GIRL MAGIC I II III

By **Destiny Skai**

WHEN A GOOD GIRL GOES BAD

By **Adrienne**

THE COST OF LOYALTY I II III

By Kweli

A GANGSTER'S REVENGE **I II III & IV**

Into the Arms of His Boss

THE BOSS MAN'S DAUGHTERS I II III IV V

A SAVAGE LOVE **I & II**

BAE BELONGS TO ME I II

A HUSTLER'S DECEIT I, II, III

WHAT BAD BITCHES DO I, II, III

SOUL OF A MONSTER I II III

KILL ZONE

A DOPE BOY'S QUEEN I II

By **Aryanna**

A KINGPIN'S AMBITON

A KINGPIN'S AMBITION **II**

I MURDER FOR THE DOUGH

By **Ambitious**

TRUE SAVAGE I II III IV V VI

DOPE BOY MAGIC I, II, III

MIDNIGHT CARTEL I II

CITY OF KINGZ

By **Chris Green**

A DOPEBOY'S PRAYER

By **Eddie "Wolf" Lee**

THE KING CARTEL **I, II & III**

By **Frank Gresham**

THESE NIGGAS AIN'T LOYAL **I, II & III**

By **Nikki Tee**

GANGSTA SHYT **I II &III**

By **CATO**

THE ULTIMATE BETRAYAL

By **Phoenix**

BOSS'N UP **I , II & III**

By **Royal Nicole**

Jamila

I LOVE YOU TO DEATH
By Destiny J
I RIDE FOR MY HITTA
I STILL RIDE FOR MY HITTA
By **Misty Holt**
LOVE & CHASIN' PAPER
By **Qay Crockett**
TO DIE IN VAIN
SINS OF A HUSTLA
By **ASAD**
BROOKLYN HUSTLAZ
By **Boogsy Morina**
BROOKLYN ON LOCK I & II
By **Sonovia**
GANGSTA CITY
By **Teddy Duke**
A DRUG KING AND HIS DIAMOND I & II III
A DOPEMAN'S RICHES
HER MAN, MINE'S TOO I, II
CASH MONEY HO'S
THE WIFEY I USED TO BE
By Nicole Goosby
TRAPHOUSE KING **I II & III**
KINGPIN KILLAZ I II III
STREET KINGS I II
PAID IN BLOOD **I II**
CARTEL KILLAZ I II III
DOPE GODS I II
By **Hood Rich**
LIPSTICK KILLAH **I, II, III**

Into the Arms of His Boss

CRIME OF PASSION I II & III

FRIEND OR FOE I II

By **Mimi**

STEADY MOBBN' **I, II, III**

THE STREETS STAINED MY SOUL

By **Marcellus Allen**

WHO SHOT YA **I, II, III**

SON OF A DOPE FIEND I II

Renta

GORILLAZ IN THE BAY **I II III IV**

TEARS OF A GANGSTA I II

3X KRAZY

DE'KARI

TRIGGADALE I II III

Elijah R. Freeman

GOD BLESS THE TRAPPERS I, II, III

THESE SCANDALOUS STREETS I, II, III

FEAR MY GANGSTA I, II, III IV, V

THESE STREETS DON'T LOVE NOBODY I, II

BURY ME A G I, II, III, IV, V

A GANGSTA'S EMPIRE I, II, III, IV

THE DOPEMAN'S BODYGAURD I II

THE REALEST KILLAZ I II

Tranay Adams

THE STREETS ARE CALLING

Duquie Wilson

MARRIED TO A BOSS... I II III

By Destiny Skai & Chris Green

KINGZ OF THE GAME I II III IV V

Playa Ray

Jamila

SLAUGHTER GANG I II III

RUTHLESS HEART I II III

By Willie Slaughter

FUK SHYT

By Blakk Diamond

DON'T F#CK WITH MY HEART I II

By Linnea

ADDICTED TO THE DRAMA I II III

INTO THE ARM OF HIS BOSS II

By Jamila

YAYO I II III

A SHOOTER'S AMBITION I II

By S. Allen

TRAP GOD I II

By Troublesome

FOREVER GANGSTA

GLOCKS ON SATIN SHEETS I II

By Adrian Dulan

TOE TAGZ I II III

By Ah'Million

KINGPIN DREAMS I II

By Paper Boi Rari

CONFESSIONS OF A GANGSTA

By Nicholas Lock

I'M NOTHING WITHOUT HIS LOVE

SINS OF A THUG

By Monet Dragun

CAUGHT UP IN THE LIFE I II III

By Robert Baptiste

NEW TO THE GAME I II III

Into the Arms of His Boss

By **Malik D. Rice**

LIFE OF A SAVAGE I II III

A GANGSTA'S QUR'AN I II

MURDA SEASON I II

GANGLAND CARTEL

By **Romell Tukes**

LOYALTY AIN'T PROMISED I II

By **Keith Williams**

QUIET MONEY I II

THUG LIFE

By **Trai'Quan**

THE STREETS MADE ME I II

By **Larry D. Wright**

THE ULTIMATE SACRIFICE I, II, III, IV, V

KHADIFI

IF YOU CROSS ME ONCE

ANGEL I II

By **Anthony Fields**

THE LIFE OF A HOOD STAR

By **Ca$h & Rashia Wilson**

THE STREETS WILL NEVER CLOSE

By **K'ajji**

CREAM

By **Yolanda Moore**

NIGHTMARES OF A HUSTLA

By **King Dream**

233

BOOKS BY LDP'S CEO, CA$H

TRUST IN NO MAN

TRUST IN NO MAN 2

TRUST IN NO MAN 3

BONDED BY BLOOD

SHORTY GOT A THUG

THUGS CRY

THUGS CRY 2

THUGS CRY 3

TRUST NO BITCH

TRUST NO BITCH 2

TRUST NO BITCH 3

TIL MY CASKET DROPS

RESTRAINING ORDER

RESTRAINING ORDER 2

IN LOVE WITH A CONVICT

LIFE OF A HOOD STAR

Into the Arms of His Boss